IT'S ALL COMING BACK TO ME NOW

Jean-Michel Fortier

IT'S ALL COMING BACK TO ME NOW

Translated by Jonathan Kaplansky

QC FICTION

Editor: Ann Marie Boulanger
Cover: Ian Sullivan Cant
Book design: Folio infographie
English proofreading: Shanti Maharaj

ISBN 978-177186-434-3 pbk
ISBN 978-1-77186-446-6 epub
ISBN 978-1-77186-447-3 pdf

Legal Deposit, 4th quarter 2026
Bibliothèque et Archives nationales du Québec
Library and Archives Canada

Published by QC Fiction, an imprint of Baraka Books

Trade Distribution & Returns
Canada – UTPdistribution.com
United States & World – Independent Publishers Group: IPGbook.com

We acknowledge the support for translation and promotion from the Société de développement des entreprises culturelles (SODEC) and the Government of Québec tax credit for book publishing administered by SODEC.

Société de développement des entreprises culturelles Québec

Financé par le gouvernement du Canada
Funded by the Government of Canada | Canada

PUBLISHED & PRINTED IN CANADA

For Céline Marie Claudette Dion

It was dead long ago
But it's all coming back to me
It's so hard to resist
And it's all coming back to me
I can barely recall
But it's all coming back to me now

Jim Steinman, "It's All Coming Back to Me Now"

1
NEW DAY

I CRACK OPEN AN EYE. It's dark in my room. This is no time to get up. They ask too much of teenagers. School should start at noon and shut down between October and March.

I reach out an arm and feel around on the floor till I put my hand on my Discman. I slip on the earphones, press Play and skip to track 15: "A New Day Has Come," original version. Piano, guitar and vocals. I wake up gently.

In the distance, my parents' slippers scrape against the linoleum in the kitchen. Across from my room, my brother is taking his shower; the light from the bathroom fills the gaps in my half-open door.

The almost six minutes the piece lasts have passed. I have time to listen to it again without missing my bus. It's a song full of confidence, miracles and walls to knock down. In the morning, Céline Dion is free to hope for something extraordinary. For me, each new day is already written. I live my life as a young Quebecer with no other goal but to move forward, leaving behind me everything that weighs heavily, that burdens me. I walk slowly. My arms are full. But one day, according to Céline and everything she stands for, I will fly away as light as air toward my destiny. At sixteen years old, you do what you can.

I fold back my duvet, yawning. In the kitchen, the smell of burnt toast lingers. My father has turned on the radio; the man from Radio-Canada wishes us a good Friday, October 10, 2003. My mother smiles and opens the newspaper, Quebec City's *Le Soleil.*

Hello, world.

2

POP DIVAS

SATURDAY. My mother has decided we have to go see Matante Pauline today. I put on my school uniform to make her happy. I don't exactly consider this an important outing, but my aunt is from another era, and she would notice if I visited her in jeans and a T-shirt. It would only emphasize the minor role she plays in our lives. I don't feel like seeing her, but I don't want to make her sad either. I ask my mother if my brother and my father are coming with us.

"Clément has a swim meet. Daniel has gone with him," she replies brusquely.

It's not that Marie-Louise wants to spend her weekend on a bench, bleary eyed, pretending to encourage her son. But still, it's not fair that Clément and my dad get out of visiting. Especially since the weather is beautiful. The maple trees are so red they seem as if they're in bloom.

The car starts and "L'aigle noir" fills the interior. It's a Marie Carmen CD, one of my mother's favourites. She hums to the best of her abilities as she backs out onto the street. She turns her head every which way to check for blind spots. Her hair is badly curled this morning, piled on top of her head. My mother does not have a nice singing voice.

I wonder if I look ridiculous wearing my school uniform on a Saturday. I should have thought of it earlier. I hope I don't run into anyone.

Matante Pauline lives in an apartment complex called the Samuel Holland. It's a 1970s superstructure made up of five or six high-rises connected by underground parking lots and a shopping plaza that has everything: restaurant, grocery store, hair salon, travel agency . . . It's not exactly a seniors' residence, but let's just say the overwhelming majority of tenants remember the Second World War. There's the Samuel Holland I, the Samuel Holland II, the Samuel Holland III, and so on. The regulars simply call it "the Samuel." I don't know which tower my aunt lives in, because once you enter, you lose all sense of direction. You go through many empty rooms, then take an elevator to the upper floors, to an apartment with a view of Quebec City.

Matante Pauline greets us warmly. "Marie-Louise and Colin. What a lovely surprise! I'm so lucky . . ."

She doesn't entertain much because she never had a husband or children. My mother is the only person who visits her from time to time. Matante Pauline is actually my great-aunt.

The apartment makes you want to sneeze. A greyish-pink carpet covers the floors. The patio door in the living room opens onto a concrete balcony where the wind will tear you to shreds. The tiny kitchen is hidden behind folding doors. I have never seen the bedroom; Matante Pauline keeps the door closed. The ceilings are stucco. It's an apartment straight out of the 1970s.

We sit down in the living room, and my mother starts talking.

"How are you, Matante?"

"I'm sick of seeing myself in the mirror."

Matante Pauline is rather large and talks about it a lot. I don't understand why her body bothers her so much. She would give anything to weigh less.

"You don't know what it's like. You're how old now, Marie-Louise? Forty-seven . . . I started gaining weight in my fifties. Before that, I was teeny tiny."

Matante says "tiny" instead of "slim," but she doesn't say "big" instead of "fat."

"But the mirror's not the worst thing. Fat people like me, with a sense of humour, we're thought of as fat comedians. Or else fat whiners. Here, at the Samuel, it's *that fat man, that fat woman.* As for me, I'm Pauline Duhaut, the fat lady on the fourteenth floor. And if I'm unlucky enough to have a cold, if I'm coughing, then I'm the stuffed-up fat lady."

I hadn't thought of that. I must admit Matante Pauline is very conscious of how she looks. My mother nods silently, her brows knitted.

"Would you like to try to lose weight?" she asks, very seriously.

"You must be joking! I'm too old to change."

Marie-Louise purses her lips. I don't know what she'd have suggested had her aunt said yes. My mother doesn't do any sports and eats whatever she likes. She's naturally thin.

When no one speaks, the apartment fills with a pleasant nothingness, the silence of a machine humming. It's coming from the vent ducts. I gaze at the Laurentians through the patio door. Matante notices.

"He's bored, poor kid. He wants to go. Are you fed up with your fat aunt, Colin?"

I don't know how to answer that. I smile stupidly, stammering "no, no." That's enough to cheer her up. No matter what I say, the moment I speak, she's happy. That's my role. My mother seizes the opportunity to change the subject.

"The last year of high school already, eh, Colin? Next year he's off to college. Do you want to tell Matante Pauline what you'll be going into?"

My stomach clenches because I don't like thinking about it. As much as I hate high school, I'm worried college will be worse. I'm an introvert.

"Probably arts and literature."

"Ah! A man of literature, like his parents. That's very good."

Pauline is a fan of the arts. The walls of the apartment are full of canvases by well-known Quebec painters. My mother tells me they're real and that there are more hidden away in Pauline's closets because there's not enough room to hang her entire collection.

The two women gossip at length about all kinds of people: cousins, sisters, aunts, acquaintances . . . I get lost in my thoughts and in a watercolour seascape hanging across from my armchair until Matante Pauline says, "What do you think of Céline Dion's new hairstyle?"

Of course, she's talking to my mother, but I straighten up, listening.

"It's nice, it suits her. Short hair looks better on her. Her face doesn't look so long."

"That's what I thought at first, too. But now, I see she's gone platinum blonde. That's not so nice; it ages her."

My mother turns to me. "Colin . . ."

I pray she's not going to say what I think she's going to say.

"Colin is a great admirer of Céline Dion. Eh, Colin? You could say you're a real fan."

Silence.

Fortunately, old Pauline doesn't realize that sixteen-year-old boys are not supposed to be interested in pop divas. She isn't surprised; she keeps going, bringing the conversation back to herself.

"Well, she's not my favourite singer. But I do think she sang very well at the Olympics."

I scoff inwardly. Matante Pauline has no cultural landmark more recent than the Atlanta Games. That was seven years ago; it's time she joined 2003.

"What did she sing, again?" she asks.

"'The Power of the Dream,'" I reply automatically.

"In any case," Pauline digresses, "she's so thin now . . . It's a shame. Such a nice voice."

My mother, who knows how much I revere Céline, gives a weak laugh that I sense is nervous. She doesn't need to worry. These kinds of comments don't affect me. Céline has every right to be blonde. Céline has every right to be thin. Matante Pauline also has every right to be fat, even if she hates herself.

She didn't notice I was wearing my school uniform.

: :

On the way home, my mother stops at the grocery store to buy honey garlic sausages.

"Your father will barbecue them!" She whispers this like a decree.

: :

Tossing the salad, my mother announces, "We went to Pauline's."

"Pauline's?" my father repeats, busy serving the sausages. He sees her so rarely that he's forgotten her.

"Pauline Duhaut!" my mother exclaims. She sounds outraged.

"Ah! Matante Pauline," my father says.

"She's not your aunt; she's mine."

"We never just call her 'Pauline,'" Clément chimes in. "We always say 'Matante Pauline.'"

"In any case, she seemed very happy to have visitors. She's aged, you know. And her apartment is full of stuff."

It's true; we had to move piles of papers that were cluttering the armchairs just so we could sit down.

"I don't know why she keeps so much stuff," my mother goes on. "Now she only has enough room on the table for her little placemat. Everything else is piles of stuff."

"What kind of stuff?"

"Envelopes, newspapers, magazines, parish bulletins, boxes, bags . . ."

My father grimaces. He detests clutter.

"Her kitchen is full of stuff, too," I add. "The oven door was open. She stores dishes in there."

My brother laughs unkindly, and I imitate him.

"It's a problem," my father declares very seriously. "It's a problem, Marie-Louise. She's getting older, and she has no children. When she leaves the Samuel Holland, who's going to get rid of it all? Imagine . . ."

My mother is getting worked up, I can tell. "I know it's a problem. I'm telling you about my afternoon, Daniel. What do you want me to do? Is it my responsibility? I'm sorry, but I don't have the time to deal with it."

My father adds fuel to the flames. "Besides, you haven't even seen her bedroom. Imagine—there must be stuff piled in there all the way to the ceiling. Good lord, Marie-Louise! What a mess."

My mother drops her fork, discouraged. My parents are always noticing problems, everywhere they look, and then they feel guilty because they can rarely solve them.

3
PORCELAIN PIERROT DOLLS

THE NEXT DAY IS SUNDAY, and I'm working. It's raining cats and dogs. I get ready to go out and wait for the bus. My mother offers to drive me to the store. I accept immediately. I take whatever's offered in terms of lifts. My mother slips on an old fluorescent coat and holey shoes. I ask her why she doesn't put on regular clothes. She answers that she's doing me a favour and I shouldn't criticize her.

As we pull into the parking lot, she announces she's going to run some errands at the pharmacy. When I remind her she's not really dressed for it, she retorts, "I'm going to the drug store, not a five-star hotel!"

::

I work in a store on chemin Sainte-Foy that sells knick-knacks. I turned sixteen in June, just before vacation, so I was able to find a summer job. I decided to keep it during the school year, too. At the knick-knack store, they only need me on

Sundays, which suits me just fine. My parents think I shouldn't work so much at my age. They don't understand my needs. I want to save money for important things, like going to see Céline Dion in Las Vegas. I don't need to study to get good grades.

Very few people come into the knick-knack store. It's a branch of a small chain of stores that is certain to go bankrupt one day. All we sell are useless thingamajigs: trinkets, Russian dolls, candles, potpourri and flowered cushions. The chain's survival depends entirely on old ladies who have coffee tables to fill with doodads. They're our only customers. There is a knick-knack store in Sainte-Foy, another one in Old Quebec and a third one in Lévis. The Sainte-Foy branch is the one that sells the least.

When I arrive, I connect to MSN, which I installed on the computer at the cash. I often kill time by chatting with my best friend, Eugénie. She makes me laugh, and the day goes by faster. Today, the manager is here. I don't understand why. On Sundays, I'm always alone in the store. It's not inventory day. She's sitting in her office, eyes narrowed at her computer screen. She has a look on her face like a scientist double-checking the calculations to launch a rocket. I need to be discreet if I want to write to Eugénie. I minimize the MSN window whenever I hear the manager approaching.

The manager of the knick-knack store is called Manon Sirois. She's the one who hired me. She started out as a simple employee and was promoted to manager less than a year ago. She seems proud of her work and her position. She's my first boss, and I'm slowly getting used to her. At the beginning of the summer, I was terrified of her. Now I understand her expectations and know which of my duties I can botch. As far as MSN is concerned, for example, she is inflexible. If she catches me chatting, I'm forced to listen to a long lecture about how it's considered time theft, which is a serious offence in the business world. I would like to take her criticism with a grain of salt, but I can't. Catherine Yao, the other student who was working this summer, didn't give a damn about the boss. I admired her insouciance. Unfortunately, the company didn't have any hours to give Catherine Yao this fall.

Manon Sirois has decided to put all the porcelain Pierrot dolls in the store on sale. She has come out of her office to explain her plan to me. That's a large quantity of merchandise to relabel. Must be why she came in today. She wants to sell off the old Pierrots to make room for the new ones she just ordered. Since I only work on Sundays, she must have come in today to give me this task. She'd rather come into the store on her day off than relabel the Pierrots herself during the week. It's a real chore for her.

The knick-knack store is located in a small strip mall on chemin Sainte-Foy. There's also a restaurant, a grocery store, a pharmacy, an orthodontist's office, a fabric store, a newsstand and a bank. Across the street, there's a hospital, which explains the large concentration of older people in the area. During my breaks, I close the shop and walk around the stores. There's nothing else to do. Eugénie's father says that a store that has to lock up while its employee takes a break does not have a bright future. He works in finance and knows his stuff. Manon Sirois could learn a lot from him.

Between two Pierrots, I chat with Eugénie. I can type very quickly, but I have to be careful. Relabeling is not computer work. If Manon Sirois hears the tapping of computer keys, she'll figure out that I'm not following her orders. Logically, she should uninstall MSN from the computer at the cash, but she doesn't know how. She probably thinks MSN is a website, and since she can't remove the internet from the computer, she thinks there's nothing she can do about it. I wriggle on my stool; disobeying makes me nervous, but it's still worth it. I can't help myself from chatting with my friend because my task is so boring.

Her: *I think I have the runs.*
Me: *LOL*
Her: *It's because of my mother's cabbage rolls.*

Me: *How old were they?*
Her: *I don't know, but I have to go again.*
Me: *Have a good shit!*
Her: *LOL*

I hear Manon Sirois shut off her computer, stand up and place her handbag on her shoulder. Quickly, I minimize the MSN window. She gives me a toothy smile and heads to the shop exit.

"Shall I leave you to it, beautiful?"

Manon Sirois never calls anyone by their first name; it's "beautiful" for boys and "gorgeous" for girls. I assume she has no memory for names.

4

THE GAME OF LIFE

FORTUNATELY, it's Thanksgiving: the school week will be shorter. I'm counting the days till Christmas. During the holidays, I forget about everything and can see whomever I like. It's the opposite of school, where I'm always running into people who know nothing about me. Hurray for the holidays. I phone Eugénie, and we decide to spend our holiday Monday at her place.

Eugénie's family is even more unusual than mine. Her mother's name is Liette, and her father is Michel. Her mother works as a medical secretary. She's good at making people feel comfortable and cracking jokes. Her father must be in big business. That's not how Eugénie talks about it, but I suspect he has a high-level position. He works at Desjardins, which is one of my favourite companies. It's entirely Quebec owned and operated.

Eugénie and her parents live on rue de Strasbourg, not far from us, in a bungalow similar to ours. Sainte-Geneviève Parish is the second poorest in Sainte-Foy. I don't think our neighbourhood seems poor. No one is begging in the streets. My father says the parish is considered poor because of avenue de Norvège, which runs alongside the Duplessis Highway. It's the only street in the neighbourhood with wall-to-wall apartment buildings. In elementary school, it was where all the foreigners lived. In my class, there was a Beninese girl, a Moroccan guy, two Senegalese, a French girl, a Mexican guy, two Chileans and four Bosnians. My father doesn't see that as a problem. But avenue de Norvège is what makes Sainte-Geneviève Parish the second poorest in Sainte-Foy.

::

Whenever I ring Eugénie's bell, the person who answers is always laughing. That's a good way to greet people. It's like the bell sets off laughter in this family.

Today, Liette opens the door. Her daughter is on the toilet. It makes them all giggle that I rang the bell at that exact moment. They tell me Eugénie shouted at them to shut the bathroom door before opening the front door. At Eugénie's house, they sometimes do their business with the door open. That's another major difference between her family and mine. I laugh with them. Everything that happens to them seems funny to me, too.

The radio in the living room is on. Céline's new song is playing: "Tout l'or des hommes." I really like it, but I'm waiting to listen to the whole album—it's coming out tomorrow—before getting carried away. I didn't *love* the one she put out in March (*One Heart*). I've become cautious. It's her first French-language record since the long break she took to have a baby. People have high hopes for this album.

Eugénie's family likes Céline Dion a lot. Not as much as I do, but enough to listen to her music and never say bad things about it. It's a very simple relationship to Céline Dion that I can't manage to have.

I chat a bit with Liette and Michel even though the music monopolizes all my attention. A song playing on the radio doesn't have the same effect as a track on an album. There's something more exciting at work. It's the result of chance. Listeners can react to what they hear. The song may spark a conversation. Even the sound is different on the radio, like the music is passing through something to reach us.

A mediocre song by Céline is always superior to anything else because she's the best singer there is. "Tout l'or des hommes" is not mediocre, but nor is it the best of the best.

: :

I go down to the basement with Eugénie.

"What do you feel like doing?"

"I don't know. You?"

My friend is never categorical about our activities. It takes her a long time to decide because she doesn't want me to be unhappy. I'm capable of being firm, but she's so considerate of my feelings that I don't dare make too much of a fuss either. That's the vicious circle of our friendship.

I propose we play *The Game of Life*, an old board game that I love. I think Eugénie finds it a bit dull, but she agrees with a smile. This girl really is an angel. We open the box, begin to set up the game. Some pieces are missing.

"None of the pieces were missing the last time. Who plays this besides us?" I ask, surprised.

She looks stunned. "I don't know. I really don't know. No idea. Really."

"You hate *The Game of Life* so much that you can't believe someone other than me wants to play."

She laughs.

We spend the afternoon chatting and playing Nintendo 64. Eugénie is a great storyteller. She imitates lots of people in her family or from school, always in the same way; the significance is not in the similarity, but in the effect. I laugh till I cry. I'm her best audience. I never get fed up listening to her. Eugénie and I are mockingbirds, as my mother would say.

: :

Back at home, I feel a bit dizzy: school tomorrow morning.

I wonder where the missing pieces of *The Game of Life* went.

5
GYM CLASS

THIS TUESDAY, we have gym class second period. It's really a nightmare, especially because this fall we're doing basketball. I can't throw the ball, and I don't even understand the game. I suspect the teacher will never explain it to us. Last week, I managed to catch a pass and tried to make a shot. But we weren't supposed to score points at that stage of the game (or from my position on the court), and Catherine Wagner let me know it. Another time, someone passed me the ball, and I passed it to someone else. Also not the right decision (at that precise moment, I should have thrown it in the hoop), as Guillaume Piché was only too pleased to shout. I looked like an idiot and don't even know why. The teacher spends a lot of time showing us how to put the ball in the hoop, which I'll never manage to do anyway, and no time teaching the rules of the game.

::

When I get to school, I go up to vomit in the fourth-floor bathroom, which is always deserted in the morning. Bits of toast from my breakfast float in the bile. Tears stream down my cheeks. When you vomit, you force so much that it makes you cry. I'm not sad—I'm used to it. It doesn't happen before every gym class; it all depends on the sport we're playing. Basketball is the worst.

Last year, I gave myself a stiff neck playing *Zelda*. I exaggerated the pain a bit, and they let me out of gym class for two weeks. That was in February, and the teacher was making us play hockey on a real skating rink. That was a narrow escape.

The first period flies by. Going down to the gym, I have a knot in my stomach, but at least I've already thrown up. That never happens twice.

In the locker room, I experience a thrill: a mixture of nerves and arousal. We always change at the same time as the guys in Group B, who are getting dressed again because they've had gym right before us, and Guillaume Brassard is in that group. He's the best-looking guy in my school. His body is different from mine—hairy legs like a man's. He even has a bit of hair around his belly button. He wears grey boxer briefs that hug his ass like a pair of girls' tights. I change close to him and check out his body as often as possible. I've never spoken to him. He's pretty quiet. He hangs out with three other guys in his group who wear glasses and spend their time in the computer room.

Gym class unfolds as usual. The teacher names Catherine Laramée and Guillaume Dionne as team captains. Two ruthless basketball players. They take turns choosing their players. Eugénie is picked around the middle of the process. She doesn't excel at anything, but she's good at everything. I envy her. I'm very strong in English, French and art, good in history and geography, average in math and science, awful in gym. The captains have chosen almost all their people; I'm the last one left, along with Catherine Julien, one of the biggest rejects of the school. Her only friends are in Grade 10, and they're all rejects, too.

It's Guillaume Dionne's turn to choose. My pits are sweating. Ugh, he picks Catherine Julien. My cheeks redden. But I should have expected it and toughen up. Catherine Julien may well be a bigger reject, but she is slightly better at basketball than I am. Catherine Laramée looks discouraged to have me on her team. I don't dare look at anyone. Every week it's the same thing. Frankly, the teacher should change his method. He doesn't see all the humiliation he causes. Gym teachers are always friends with the athletic students. That's problematic behaviour.

I don't know why the others take the sport so seriously. It's not like basketball is going to repair the hole in the ozone layer.

::

I go to a private school with barely five hundred students in a snobbish part of the city. I thought I'd like it when I took the tour, in sixth grade. My brother went to a big public high school. But that intimidated me. The idea of this small private school made me feel safe. But now that I think about it, it may be worse than the public high school.

It was a boarding school for boys until recently. Now they accept girls, but sports take centre stage, and there isn't much else to do. Not even a music class. I chose my high school poorly. Had I known you had to play football or soccer to have a good experience, I would have gone somewhere else. But no one told me. I might not have even noticed if my mother hadn't pointed it out, last year, after learning that the school was planning to build another gymnasium on the grounds. She couldn't suppress a sarcastic exclamation when I told her that. Marie-Louise holds music and the arts in high esteem.

Later, I heard her saying to my father disapprovingly, "That school doesn't really encourage students with diverse interests." She was right. It's not like that everywhere. At the public high school, there's a balance. They even put on a show at the end of the year at the local theatre. My small private school would never do that. Now I realize that I've wasted my time at a school for jocks. I have regrets.

High school isn't a problem if you're slim, athletic and studious, like Catherine Wagner, or a tall, popular pothead, like Guillaume Piché. Or even if you're Eugénie, the nice, curly-haired girl who doesn't bother anybody.

::

Eugénie joins me in line at the cafeteria. We don't have gym again till next week, so I'll be able to relax a bit. I don't talk about it to my friend. She knows how much I hate it, but there's nothing else to say. I just have to put up with it until June. In college, we can choose our gym class. Not ideal, but better than nothing. Apparently, you can take an archery class in college. I can't believe I'd be as bad at archery as I am at basketball.

The cafeteria ladies know everyone. They greet the students by name. Former inmates, according to Eugénie's father. One of them seems completely fed up with her job and never smiles. I understand her, but she should act professional. We're her customers. As Manon Sirois says, the customer is always right.

The cafeteria's chicken burgers are to die for.

::

The day is over, and I take the city bus home with Eugénie. Sometimes we talk. Sometimes we listen to music. This afternoon, I slip on my headphones, leave the Discman in my bag and press Play. Today, it's *S'il suffisait d'aimer*—an excellent album that I almost prefer to *D'eux*.

There are no other students from our school on the bus. I sit quietly with Eugénie. Céline sings "En attendant ses pas," and I daydream.

6
ENGLISH

ON TOP OF THEIR DAILY ENGLISH CLASSES, all Group As in the school have one day of immersion per cycle. That means that about once a week, we do only English from morning till afternoon. The immersion program means we lose out on a few French, math and science classes, and we have to learn the same concepts as Group B in less time. It isn't a very big challenge for me, but I know there are other students who struggle. Catherine Pronovost, for example, is mediocre in English. Last year, she almost went down to Group B.

English is my favourite subject. Not everything is bleak at my small private school.

According to the adults, English is the most important thing you can learn in your life. They all say that because of globalization. I can't explain globalization, but it's new and it's a good thing. Thanks to globalization, English will open up all the doors for us, the doors being jobs. Manon Sirois speaks poor English, which explains why she's the manager of a knick-knack store.

Eugénie is a little less gifted than I am in English, but she gets by. We're both going to enrol in English-language college. That choice is supposed to open even more doors for us. Eugénie will study science. That's the big difference between her and me. I don't like science. After English, the subject that opens the most doors is science. Eugénie will soon find herself in front of a billion open doors.

I'd like to go into a field that pays well, but I've decided to do arts and literature instead. I can't really see myself studying something else. I feel like it's a bad choice. But my parents are supportive.

"The important thing is that you do what you enjoy," they say.

It's nice of them, but they also studied literature, and now they work for the provincial government. That's not the type of life that appeals to me. Eugénie's father works for Desjardins, a finance company. Private companies offer more interesting career opportunities than government. Fortunately, English will open a ton of doors for me.

7
SCRATCHED FLOORS

MY BROTHER WANTS TO PLAN A PARTY, but at our house that's not allowed: no house parties, ever. My parents are afraid the teenagers will demolish the house and the neighbours will call the police because of the noise. Personally, I don't care: Eugénie is my only friend, and a party for two is pointless. But for Clément, it's a grave injustice. All his friends have them, and he feels left out. This evening, at the table, he presents solid arguments that my father shoots down one by one.

"Do you want me to be the reject who never has parties?"

"You're not a reject. You have fifty-six friends that you talk about all the time."

"My fifty-six friends will think you have something to hide."

"Then feel free to invite them to dinner to prove we don't."

"Guillaume Poirier's parents let him have parties at their place and everything is fine."

"Guillaume Poirier's parents have an old house with scratched floors."

"I'll never get a girlfriend if I don't throw a party."

"Help Guillaume Poirier give his next one—the girls will be throwing themselves at you."

"I'm turning eighteen in two weeks, and it's the only thing I'm asking you for!"

"Well . . ."

This last argument seems to have hit home. Daniel falls silent and looks up at Marie-Louise. If there's anything my parents respect, it's birthdays. For them, it's important to mark the passage of time and celebrate milestones. Eighteen years is a big deal. That's when you become an adult.

It feels like the wind is about to change. Clément holds his breath as he chews a mouthful of spaghetti.

My mother breaks the silence. "We'll think about it."

I'm shocked. Clément, too. He doesn't say anything else.

My father sighs. "When would your party be?"

"Saturday."

My mother gives a start. "This Saturday? Clément, today is Wednesday!"

"But the following Saturday is my real birthday, and I know you'll want to have a family dinner."

My father raises his hand and repeats, "We'll think about it."

They're going to agree. With my parents, the smallest opening is a pathway to victory. Their "thinking" always plays out in our favour. Clément must be thrilled. Personally, I couldn't care less.

8

THE WORLD IS FAKE

EUGÉNIE AND I are sitting at the kitchen table with a package of Fig Newtons. My mother is wandering around the house with a mop. She passes through the kitchen from time to time and, while she's at it, swipes some cookies from us. It's Friday evening. My brother has gone out, and my father is washing the dinner dishes. I tell Eugénie about a pathetic scene I witnessed at school.

"So Guillaume Piché stood there in front of Catherine Julien's locker and blocked her from taking out her stuff, just to piss her off."

"Who is Catherine Julien?" asks my father, who is not supposed to be listening to this clearly private conversation.

I roll my eyes. "Dad, it's none of your business!"

He doesn't care. "Is she the girl we gave a lift to during a snowstorm last year? She seemed nice."

It was indeed her, but I want to shut him up, so I reply, "No! That wasn't her. Catherine Julien is a reject."

My mother breezes past the table. "Really, Colin," she interjects. "She's a human being."

Eugénie bursts out laughing.

"Ugh, Mom. No, she's the school weirdo," I reply.

"That's no reason to be mean to her," my father says. "I hope you're not one of those people who ostracize her, Colin."

"No, I've never in my life been mean to her. I just talk about her behind her back. Let me tell Eugénie my story!"

My parents fall silent, and I go on. "So Guillaume Piché was bugging Catherine Julien by blocking her locker, and then who should appear out of nowhere? Catherine Crosnier!"

Eugénie lets out a cry of surprise. I continue. "And then, madame starts defending Catherine Julien, threatening to go get the monitor . . ."

My father interrupts me. "That's good. That's the right thing to do."

I burst out laughing. Eugénie smiles discreetly. "No, but Mr. Bourque," she explains to my father. "It's because Catherine Crosnier has been laughing at Catherine Julien since Grade 7. She's no better than us."

"Catherine Crosnier is so fake," I add. "I've never seen anyone do something so fake. Who does she think she is?"

My father still doesn't get it. "Just because she behaved badly in the past doesn't mean she can't change."

My father's so naive. Did he ever go to high school?

"Dad, she's a fake. Catherine Crosnier is a total fake. In Grade 9, she sprained her ankle at badminton and spent the whole winter on crutches. Everyone knew she was faking, even the gym teacher. Then one Monday morning, she showed up at school without the crutches, her ankle just fine, no explanation, like there was nothing wrong. I was freaking out. We all were."

Eyes focused on the dishwater, my father lets a few seconds go by. "In any case, she's the only one who did the right thing."

I don't say anything else, but Eugénie and I exchange a series of meaningful looks: people are fake. End of discussion.

9

WEIRD AND POTENTIALLY SEXUAL

THIS EVENING THERE'S AN HISTORIC EVENT taking place on avenue de Cherbourg: the very first house party. It's a turning point. Clément has invited about fifteen friends from his college. The guests are restricted to the basement and the kitchen. My father even posted a notice on the door between the kitchen and the living room:

Off limits except in case of emergency

He and Marie-Louise will spend the evening in front of the TV. The party ends at midnight. Clément thinks that's pathetic and not a real party if it finishes so early, but he has no choice. It's that or nothing.

The house is buzzing with action. My father and brother push the basement furniture up against the walls. Clément moves his stereo system downstairs with all his CDs. I ask him what music he'll play.

"Linkin Park and Eminem."

I was going to suggest songs by Céline Dion and Jennifer Lopez. "Treat Her Like a Lady" could almost pass for rap or reggae. "Make You Happy," too. "Unison" is dance music. Or "Je danse dans ma tête" or "Des mots qui sonnent." Céline has lots of songs you can dance to. And that's all Jennifer Lopez does: party songs. But my brother would have laughed at me. I was wise to keep my ideas to myself.

::

I've invited Eugénie to sleep over so I won't be bored. Since the party is making a terrible racket, I have no issue playing loud music in my room. I'd like to listen to Céline's new album (*1 fille & 4 types*) because it just came out and I don't yet know all the songs by heart, but I know Eugénie prefers the diva's greatest hits, so I put on *All the Way . . . A Decade of Song* to make her happy. I'm just glad I have a friend who doesn't judge my music.

After a while, I want to do something else. Eugénie suggests we join my parents in the living room. They've rented *Swimming Pool*, a French film that seems weird to me and potentially sexual. I think it's rated PG-13. I really don't want to watch it with Marie-Louise and Daniel, but I can't come up with a better idea. My parents are happy to see us.

The movie is about a woman who moves into a country house to write a novel and is constantly disrupted by a sexually uninhibited young girl. Everything is fine at first. I even find the film interesting. Then, just as I'm beginning to relax, the girl starts sucking a guy's penis next to the pool. You don't see anything, but it's very obvious what's happening, and it's too much for me. Who knows how far this film will go? I feel myself blush and I stand up, carefully avoiding eye contact with my parents. Eugénie doesn't follow me.

I hide out in the kitchen, where I pour myself a glass of juice, adjusting my briefs through my pants to hide my erection. The counter is full of half-empty glasses that smell like fruity alcohol. The sound of girls shouting and boys laughing reaches me from the basement. The last thing I want to do is keep watching my parents' porn movie. I venture onto the staircase.

Sitting halfway down, I can't see much. It's dark, and the stereo system is blaring disgusting music. It's like no one is there: Clément and his friends must all be in the other room. I'm about to go back up to the kitchen when a voice emerges from the darkness.

"Are you Clément's brother?"

I stifle a cry, almost fall down the stairs. The only thing I can think of to say is, "Who's there?"

"It's me."

I hear the rubbing of his socks on the carpet. Then he's standing in front of the staircase, five steps below me. The distant glow from the kitchen falls on him, revealing his face.

He's the most gorgeous guy I've ever seen.

10

A NEW SCALE

TWO, THREE, FOUR SECONDS PASS, and I'm no longer living in this world. I don't know how my lungs are still rising and falling—I feel so removed from my parents' fucked-up film, from my hand resting on the banister, from the weight of my body on the ground, from everything surrounding me and everything I experienced before.

"I'm Yann."

He's Yann. Yann watches me, remaining in full control of himself: I'm not like him, handsome enough to frame. Who would be breathless at the sight of me? I don't know what to say; he's a guest of my brother's, a friend of my brother's, one of my brother's party guests. My brain cells are exploding, my thoughts sinking and drowning before reaching me.

"I'm Yann. And you?"

He's asking me a question; he's waiting for an answer; he's staring at me. Does he seem serious? Is he laughing? In the dim light, I can't unlock the mystery of his expression.

With a lump in my throat, I murmur hoarsely, "Colin."

"Nice to meet you, Colin."

He doesn't look like anyone I know; he's as handsome as Jack in *Titanic*. On a scale from one to Guillaume Brassard, he bursts through the stratosphere. I'll have to change the scale; I need a new scale immediately.

"Yann who?"

I just asked him his last name, like an idiot who plans to scour the phone book for his address. His face is about to contort as he slowly realizes my insignificance—me, the semi-reject of Grade 11, and him, the cool college guy.

But no, it looks like he's preparing to smile. His mouth opens and it's in my direction that he curls his lips, revealing teeth biting the tip of his tongue. He's so cute. I think I love him; I already love him more than my mother, my father, my brother and Eugénie.

"Yann Moreau."

A scale from one to Yann Moreau. My sky has just expanded.

11

THE FIRST TIME EVER I SAW YOUR FACE

CLÉMENT'S FRIENDS left at the stroke of midnight: my father went down to flash the lights and turn off the music. Nothing bad happened, which is good. Maybe Clément can plan a rave when he turns twenty.

Eugénie is sleeping on a mattress on the floor next to my bed. Before turning out the lights, I removed the Discman from my backpack. I'm listening to "The First Time Ever I Saw Your Face" by Céline on repeat. It's the most beautiful love song in her repertoire. I grab my journal, my pen and a flashlight, and I translate the song lyrics. I reread the verse and find it beautiful and touching, like I'm the one who composed it:

La toute première fois que j'ai vu ton visage
J'ai cru que le soleil se levait dans tes yeux
Que la lune et les étoiles
Étaient tes offrandes à l'obscurité
Et aux cieux infinis
Mon amour

The first time ever I saw your face
I thought the sun rose in your eyes
And the moon and the stars
Were the gifts you gave
To the dark and the endless skies
My love

My whole body is bathed in sweat just thinking about my conversation with Yann Moreau. It hadn't lasted more than three minutes, but already those minutes are the most important ones of my existence. Yann Moreau is on the same swim team as my brother. He's studying social science, not math. He's thinking about doing a bachelor's degree in film studies, but that's not offered in Quebec City. He'll have to go to Montreal. That's what I found out this evening.

Before today, if you'd wanted to make a movie about the key moments in my life, there would have been nothing to show. Now, the movie would be three minutes long.

12
ALL THE PUPPETS

I CAN'T GET OVER IT. When I get to work again this Sunday, I don't even have to unlock the place; Manon Sirois is sitting in her office, eyes riveted to the computer screen.

"Good morning, beautiful!"

And I thought I'd have peace and quiet to think about Yann Moreau.

"Beautiful, when you've put down your bag, would you bring me all the puppets in the store?"

As if the Pierrots weren't enough, now she wants to order a new batch of puppets. Her timing is bad today. Since last night, I've had a bingo machine pinging in my stomach. I practically didn't sleep a wink. I need all my time, all my energy to think about Yann Moreau. This is the first time someone's turned my world upside down. Even Guillaume Brassard doesn't have the same effect on me when he strips off his underwear in the locker room. I'm experiencing something, for once. As for Manon Sirois, she has eyes only for her puppets.

"I want you to put them all on sale for me, beautiful. I've just placed a huge order for new puppets. I can't believe I'll be alone when it comes in this week. If the old ones are already relabelled, that'll be a big help."

I'm sure Manon Sirois is doing her best, but her work really seems like a mountain for her. My tasks are dead boring, but they're obviously not insurmountable. Being manager of a knick-knack shop is certainly more stressful than being a simple salesperson. But whatever—I have an urgent need to think about Yann Moreau. Not about discounted puppets.

::

It's almost two o'clock and Manon Sirois is still hanging around in her office, her eyes round, her face glued to the screen. Was she bored at home? Why is she coming to work on Sundays now? Nothing is forcing her to come manage the relabelling of puppets. I know almost nothing about her, and she doesn't know me either. My father says he's seen her coming out of an apartment building in the Campanile area. Campanile is a neighbourhood full of old people. As if she doesn't see enough of them at the knick-knack store. I'm sure she's never experienced anything approaching what I feel for Yann Moreau. Manon Sirois is not unpleasant, but I can't picture her with a family, with a husband and children. Is she a lesbian? I have an absurd urge to talk to her about Yann Moreau, but the thought of that getting back to my parents paralyzes me. If they find out, I'll die. My secret love.

An old lady enters the shop. If I have to serve customers on top of taking care of the puppets, I'll really have no time to think about Yann Moreau!

13

GAGGING

TODAY, Catherine Crosnier, Miss Fake herself, fainted—for real—right in the middle of French class.

I've never passed out, but it doesn't look restful because when she came to, she announced that she felt sick to her stomach. Everyone stepped back, even the teacher, Ms. Trudel. Catherine Crosnier looked at her imploringly. "I'm sorry," she whimpered.

I must admit she looked pitiful. The monitor, who used to be a prison guard, arrived at that point to take her to the nurse's office.

We all sat back down, and I presumed Ms. Trudel would carry on with her class, but then she clutched at her chest, exclaimed that she felt sick, too, and half-ran out of the class. The girls' bathroom is right across the hall from our classroom, so everyone could hear her gagging as she vomited. Catherine Pronovost went "Ugh!" and Guillaume Piché laughed. Since I'm a frequent puker myself, other people's barfing doesn't have the slightest effect on me.

Finally, Ms. Trudel returned to class, eyes and nose red. She began to ramble. You could tell she was just waiting for the bell to ring so she could go home. Instead of resuming teaching, she started telling us a story about her sister who is diabetic and moved to Magog. It was extremely interesting but totally unrelated to French class. In high school, teachers regularly draw on their personal lives to kill time. This time, Ms. Trudel had just vomited in the bathroom, which was a valid excuse to recount what she described as "a slice of life." I don't like that expression: it makes me think of roast beef.

::

Catherine Crosnier is one of the lucky students who live very close to school. Usually, she walks home. But today, a black car is waiting for her outside the building. The secretary must have told her parents their daughter fainted.

Catherine Crosnier climbs into the car just as Eugénie and I are walking out of school to wait for the bus. And who should be sitting in the front passenger seat of said car?

Yann Moreau.

My lungs deflate. Is it him? It's him. His brown mop of hair is tousled like he's just come from the pool. The warm autumn light turns his skin golden. I make out three freckles on his cheek. His little head is perfect.

I want him to see me and for something to happen. Anything—a start, a smile or a wink. He has to see me. I start walking around the car to cross the lane. It's in the opposite direction from the bus stop, so of course Eugénie is confused.

"Hey, where are you going?"

Shut up, Eug, I think. Just let me walk casually in front of the Volvo. Let Yann notice me, recognize me, lower his window, say my name, know that I exist in the world, that I'm carrying a black backpack and wearing a dumb private school uniform, that I have pimples on my cheeks but blue eyes and good general knowledge!

Nothing. Mr. Crosnier waits for me to pass, starts up the car, and drives away. The stupid reflections of the trees lining the lane prevent me from locking eyes with Yann Moreau through the car window. I don't even know if he saw me. Eugénie joins me.

"He looks cool," she says, "Catherine Crosnier's brother."

"If he's her brother, why don't they have the same last name?"

"Oh, you know him?"

I blush. "No."

"Then how do you know he doesn't have the same last name as Catherine?"

Shut up, Eug. You shut up, too, Colin. My friend is waiting for an answer that doesn't come.

She shrugs. “If his last name isn’t Crosnier, then he must be her stepbrother.”

Catherine Crosnier is Yann Moreau’s stepsister.

I look at my best friend, both grateful for her insight and outraged by her uselessness. Why couldn’t *she* be my crush’s stepsister? Why am I wasting my time with Eugénie Bujold? No, I’m losing my mind; Eugénie is a great friend. But I can’t help it; everything is getting on my nerves. It must be one of the symptoms of love.

14

THEY LOOK LIKE BUGS

SETTLED IN FRONT OF THE TV, I hear the car doors slam and the raised voices of my parents. It sounds like they're bickering, but as soon as they walk in, I realize they're laughing. Good-naturedly, even. Especially my mother.

She walks into the living room holding a big bouquet of birds of paradise.

"Hello, my prince!"

On Friday nights, she's often in a good mood, but this is unusual, even for her. I mutter a greeting and decide to ignore her. I'm too hungry for joyfulness. On TV, it's a boring scene where two characters are arguing. I stare at it like my life depends on it.

"You're not going to ask me what I'm doing with a bouquet of flowers?"

She waves the flowers wrapped in cellophane in front of me, the plastic crackling. I roll my eyes and snap, "You can tell me during the commercials!"

Marie-Louise steps out of her happy bubble to shoot back, "Great! Nice way to start the evening!

Forget it, then. We're eating at Pacini. Be ready in twenty minutes."

: :

At the table in the restaurant, my mother relates in great detail the story of her birds of paradise. We didn't even have to ask; it was obvious she was dying to tell us. My brother is sitting far back and hunched over in the booth but still listening with interest. On Friday nights, he's always torn. Since we often eat at Pacini or Tangville and he likes a free meal, he comes with us, but then he spends the whole time tapping his feet impatiently because he just wants to go meet his friends at a party somewhere.

In short, my mother has a secret admirer. The bouquet was on her desk when she returned from lunch. She asked all her colleagues in the department, but no one could tell her who left it there. But it put her in an excellent mood.

Next to her, my father is listening to the story for the second time, smiling. I'm stunned. I can't get over the fact that my mother, with her mop of curly hair, is being hit on at work. She doesn't even wear dresses!

"Anyway, he doesn't know you well. Birds of paradise . . . They don't even look like real flowers. They look like bugs."

Daniel is right: Marie-Louise far prefers carnations or simple daisies.

"Maybe it's your boss," I suggest.

My mother pretends to pass out. "Good lord! Not him!"

Everyone laughs. "Maybe it's a woman," Clément chimes in. "A government lady who's crazy about you."

I look down at my lasagna. My father says something I don't want to hear, and he and my mother crack a few jokes. I don't like the turn this conversation has taken and slip out to the washroom.

When people start talking about *that* subject, I disappear, like a large spring has ejected me elsewhere. Today, at sixteen, if someone dared ask me the question directly, I'd be totally incapable of denying it. And I don't understand why, because even the thought of admitting it makes my blood run cold. I'm not ready, and I don't want people to know or guess it. But lying about it exhausts me. I'm stuck. So I avoid the subject.

On the toilet, I think for a long while about Yann Moreau while a vague sadness settles in my belly.

15

SUPERHEROINE

CÉLINE DION AND I are embroiled in a great love affair. It's been going on for a long time. It's a bit of a secret. My first secret love.

At eight years old, I came across the cassette of *The Colour of My Love* while rummaging through my parents' things. I borrowed my father's old Walkman and wore out the tape. My obsession was born from "The Power of Love," a seminal ballad that I must have listened to ten thousand times before understanding a damned line.

Then came *D'eux*, which my parents bought on CD. It took me some time to fall in love with it because I was used to hearing Céline Dion in English; that's how I'd discovered her. In French, Céline topped the charts, but for me, nothing will ever surpass her English-language albums of the nineties. I spent the end of my elementary school years revelling in the incomparable *Falling into You* and *Let's Talk About Love*, in that order. When *S'il suffisait d'aimer* came out, I wanted to give it a chance—the song "On ne change pas" had captivated me—and from there, I ended up going back to *D'eux* and discovering the extraordinary *Dion chante Plamondon* and then *Incognito*, and then everything else.

Céline is the most reliable person I know. She doesn't sing off-key. She never runs out of breath or power. She's a pro who works long hours and spares no effort. The recording sessions for the album *Let's Talk About Love* prove what she's capable of. She pulls off the most dizzying vocal feats with no sweat; everything is within her range. On "The Reason," she strains her vocal cords with a smile.

Céline is versatile. She can be solemn, light, crass, elegant, serious, funny, abrasive, silky. And just like her, her voice can be sparkling, coarse, dark, ethereal, thundering. I know her repertoire well enough to pick out my favourite inflections and play them over and over, in two- or three-second clips: my ears can never get enough. I no longer hear the voice of a woman but the abstraction of a musical instrument—a piano, a bell, or a flute. A one-woman band.

On days when everything goes wrong, I watch my VHS tape of *Live à Paris*. During "Prière païenne," I hold my breath for the singer on stage at the Zénith, working the crowd, running a half-marathon, hitting the most piercing notes on the scale. On the choruses of "River Deep,

Mountain High," and "Le blues du businessman," her voice resonates so loudly it's like she has an amplifier in her belly. Swept away by her energy, I dissolve before this powerful woman, in perfect control of her body and her voice, who sings like a superheroine, hair short, clad in black leather from head to toe. Céline believes everything is possible and sweeps me up in her dream.

Hollywood made her its designated singer. Four of her songs have been nominated for Oscars, and two have won. Music is marvellous, film is magical, but there's nothing better than film music. Whenever Céline sings at the Oscars, I record the ceremony and pause on the image of Tom Hanks, Jim Carrey or Meryl Streep clapping for her. Each of her successes belongs to me a little.

Céline's music speaks to me. Her voice pierces my armour and reaches a place that does not exist without her, a heart that she invented just for me. I realize she'll never know me, but she's singing directly to me. Her songs resonate so deep inside me that I have no choice but to believe that. To doubt it would be too painful.

Normal boys do not listen to Céline Dion.

But when she stares straight into the camera and makes her vocal cords vibrate powerfully enough to raise the theatre roof, Céline inspires me to not give a damn.

16

A PERPLEXING OBJECT

AT THE KNICK-KNACK STORE, we sell the Heart of the Ocean (the big heart-shaped pendant that the old lady in *Titanic* throws into the water at the end of the movie).

Of course it's fake. Besides, it's not even well made. You can tell right away that it's smaller and not as cleanly cut as the original. But Manon Sirois still keeps it locked up in a glass cabinet. It costs fifty-nine ninety-nine.

I've been working at the knick-knack store for almost six months, and no one has ever asked me to see it. People walk by it and ask, "Is that the necklace from *Titanic*?"

I answer them, nodding my head dully. I have no clue why the store where I work sells a replica of this famous jewel.

From time to time, when the small strip mall that houses the knick-knack store is completely deserted, I take the Heart of the Ocean from its display case and examine it. It looks cheap up close, but it still sets off my imagination. I'd really like to try it on, but I don't dare.

In 1998, Céline Dion wore the Heart of the Ocean, the real one, to the Academy Awards. She sang "My Heart Will Go On" and pounded her chest. The next day on the radio, I heard a DJ say she looked like a Coke bottle in her navy blue sheath dress. I thought she'd looked divine.

I don't know if the Heart of the Ocean that we sell at the knick-knack store should be considered a normal piece of jewellery or part of a Halloween costume. In any case, no one seems to want it. Even the real one—the one that's worth a fortune—no one wants. In an interview on *The Rosie O'Donnell Show*, Céline said she'd never buy anything like it because she wouldn't know what to do with it.

It's a perplexing object.

17

LIKE I NO LONGER EXIST

MY BROTHER HAS HIS FIRST GIRLFRIEND. In any case, the first one he's talked about and wants to introduce to us. He's invited her over for dinner. It's Saturday, and my mother has lots of time to cook something delicious. There's a fat, grain-fed chicken in the oven that's been cooking all afternoon, filling the house with a wonderful aroma.

The first snow has fallen. Outside the window, everything is white. It made me happy, and I immediately started listening to *These Are Special Times*. Christmas goes by so quickly. Might as well make the most of the time leading up to it. No one sings Christmas better than Céline Dion, except for maybe the great Mariah Carey, but I don't want to get into that debate.

I'm excited. What does Clément's girlfriend look like? I hope she has long hair.

I have a hard time judging my brother's attractiveness. He's a swimmer, so he has an athlete's body. Yann Moreau also swims, but Yann Moreau has the sexy face of a certain Titanic passenger, which is ironic for a swimmer. My brother has my father's face. I have my mother's.

⁚⁚

My brother's girlfriend arrived around six o'clock, just as my mother was taking the chicken out of the oven. She's short and blonde and answers politely to everything you say to her. Politeness is nice, but it's super boring and doesn't mean anything. I hope one day she finds her personality, if she has one.

She sat in my usual spot: we're off to a good start! I had to sit at the end of the table, a very unusual place for me. Might as well go have dinner at the neighbours' house. No one tells her not to sit in my chair. It's like I no longer exist.

Marie-Louise serves her a slice of white meat with potatoes and peas.

"Oh, that's too much! I'll never eat all that!" my brother's girlfriend exclaims.

I peer at her plate. There really isn't that much. What a faker. Or she's covering her ass in case she finds it revolting; she could blame it on her bird-like appetite. I understand, because other families' cooking turns my stomach.

She introduced herself to everyone when she arrived: Catherine. As my mother hands me my plate, I ask her last name.

"Moreau."

An electric current runs through me.

"Yeah, Catherine is my friend Yann's sister," Clément specifies. "He swims with me. He brought her to my birthday party, and that's how we met."

I can't believe it. I'm crazy about Yann Moreau, and Clément is infatuated with his sister. There are a million Catherines in Quebec City, and he had to choose Catherine Moreau. But Yann is different. There's no one else like him in the world.

My father, who is interested in only two things, asks, "And how old are you, Catherine?"

"I'm twenty."

"Are you in school?"

She's in the middle of taking a long drink of water, so everyone has to wait for her to answer, which adds to the dramatic effect when she says quietly, "I've just started medical school."

Oh my . . . A future doctor! The perfect profession, the perfect life. Getting rich while helping people. I'm impressed. My brother has found someone better than him.

: :

Clément and his girlfriend have gone to a party somewhere. My innards writhe in jealousy at the thought that they might meet up with Yann Moreau, but I can't say anything or follow them. They would never agree to me tagging along, and my parents think I'm too young, at sixteen, to go to the same places as my brother.

In the living room, in front of the TV with my parents, I say innocently, "Clément's girlfriend is cool. She's going to be a doctor!"

"Yes . . ." my father replies unenthusiastically, without looking up from his magazine.

When he sees my puzzled expression, he adds, "No, it's good, but well . . . As long as she's doing what she likes and gets something out of it . . . She seems nice, but that has nothing to do with her being a med student. She could be studying welding, and that would be fine with me."

Good lord, but my father is contrary! Seriously, his son's girlfriend is a future doctor, bound to bring honour and prosperity to us all. That's not nothing. My parents lack ambition.

Yann Moreau's family seems perfect—aside from the stepsister, Catherine Crosnier, the fake. I can't believe Clément is dating a Moreau. When that's all I want. If I end up dating Yann Moreau one day, we'll look like a bunch of weirdos, brothers and sisters who paired up. Not cool. I almost hope it doesn't last between Clément and Catherine Moreau.

But what am I going on about? I'll never date Yann.

18

BROWN MAKEUP

THIS SUNDAY, at the knick-knack store, I really thought I'd be left alone. I'd opened the shop calmly, turned on the computer, connected to MSN. Ahead of me stretched long, empty hours, an ideal day to think about Yann Moreau's pretty face.

But around noon, who should appear in the store? Manon Sirois. The second I see her, I know something is going on. Her eyes are gleaming like she just put in drops, and she's carrying her bag awkwardly on her shoulder.

"Excuse me, Colin!" she exclaims.

Then she rushes into her office. I stay seated at the cash. Next, I hear her breathing loudly like she's crying. I don't know what to do. I'm so taken aback that I didn't even think to close the MSN window on the computer.

Eugénie is better than I am at helping people. I write to her:

SOS! My boss is bawling all alone in her office and I don't know why!

She doesn't reply immediately. Is she doing it on purpose? Manon Sirois sniffs even more intensely. I'm stressed out.

Finally:

Her: *Well, go in and see her.*
Me: *No way!*
Her: *Yes way.*

That wasn't what I wanted to read. Eugénie should have advised me to silently pick up my bag and my coat, leave the shop and never set foot there again. That's what a real friend would have done.

Me: *What am I supposed to say? I don't want to talk to her!*
Her: *Ask her if she needs anything.*

Damn, life is complicated. My best friend is adamant:

You have no choice but to go and see her.
It's too weird if you ignore her.

Reluctantly, I stand up, knocking my boots against the metal of the stool so Manon hears me coming. I stand in her office doorway and glance inside. She's sitting in front of her computer screen, head in her hands, her back turned to me. I decide to give her a choice.

"Do you want to talk, or would you rather be alone?"

Hearing my voice, she gives a start and looks at me. Her brown eye makeup has run down her cheeks, creating little dots.

"No, it's okay!"

What does that mean? It's unclear. I back up a few steps. As far as I'm concerned, I did what I had to do, and now I can leave. A lady her age doesn't want to confide in a teenager.

But Manon Sirois continues speaking. "It's my mother. They found a spot on her lung." Her voice catches. She covers her face with her hands. "Do you realize what that means, Colin?"

I realize her mother must be a very old lady who smokes. "That doesn't necessarily mean it's serious . . ." I reply.

She must think I'm a moron. But I think I'm right. Nodding, she takes out a Kleenex from her purse and blows her nose three times. "I'm sorry, Colin. Please excuse me."

"No, no, it's fine. You don't have to apologize."

As I utter this, I realize how banal my words are. Sometimes I feel like I'm reciting lines straight out of a cheesy soap opera. Manon, too, perhaps, realizes that I'm the wrong person to console her. She picks up her handbag, apologizes again and leaves the store.

The real drama this Sunday is not the spot on Manon Sirois' mother's lung; it's that she came looking for comfort here, at the knick-knack store, from her sixteen-year-old employee.

19

RATHER EXTRAORDINARY

SOMETIMES, on the weekend, Marie-Louise, Daniel, Clément and I end up in front of the TV at the same time. If we're lucky, we catch a quiz show on one of the local networks.

The host asks questions, and we try to answer before the contestants do. Clément and I are pretty bad. But my parents know a lot. My father, who doesn't watch much television, reads the newspaper during the show. In the rare case my mother draws a blank, she calls out to him:

"Daniel, the Plantagenets—was that in England?"

"Daniel, who wrote *Death in Venice* again?"

"Daniel, what's the capital of Sudan?"

My father looks up, furrows his brow, hesitates for two seconds and gives an answer: usually the right one. And the entire Bourque family shouts triumphantly, "Yes!"

I often tell my parents they should send in their names for the TV quiz shows, but they don't want anything to do with Quebec game shows.

"In Quebec, quiz shows pay peanuts. They don't have the budget because general knowledge isn't valued here like it is in France. Imagine, a grand prize of a hundred and fifty bucks . . ."

I enjoy this snobbery. It makes me believe I come from a good family. I feel rather extraordinary. My parents might not have grand career ambitions, but I tell myself that if they tried, they could accomplish anything.

20

FOURTEEN CHARMS

MANON SIROIS HAD A CARELESS ACCIDENT. She fell on the steps of her building and broke a bunch of bones. It'll be a long recovery. She smokes, and she's not very strong.

They've sent Linda Beaudoin, the assistant manager of the knick-knack shop in Lévis, as her temporary replacement. Just this once, she's come into work this Sunday to meet me. You can tell by her face that she's pissed off about having to cross the bridge to come manage me.

Today, the time passes even slower than in gym class. I've dusted half the displays and returned to sit behind the cash. Eugénie is not on MSN; she went out with her parents. If I had Yann Moreau's email address, I could add him to my contacts, but that would be too big a move. He'd find it weird and tell my brother about it.

I lean on the counter, head in my hands. Linda suddenly appears from Manon Sirois' office, where she's been pretending to work; she's sipping a Red Bull. It's the first time I've met someone who walks around carrying a can with a straw in it. She stands in front of me, stretches and sighs her cherry breath right in my face.

"Boring as hell, eh?"

I give her a sympathetic pout. She goes in the back and soon reappears with her purse. Fourteen charms—I counted them—hang off it and click violently whenever she moves.

"Look, I bought this at Galeries Chagnon."

She takes a CD out of her bag. *One Heart*, Céline's latest English-language album, released six months ago.

"Personally, I'm not really crazy about her, but I heard her song on the radio, you know, 'Drive All Night' . . ."

I bite my lip; I do everything I can to hold back, but I just can't. I morph into a mini teacher. "Actually, it's 'I Drove All Night.'"

She doesn't even look at me, her face buried in her purse sorting Kleenexes. "Huh? I like this album. It's got more of a beat; it's the kind of thing they'd play in a bar."

She grabs the plastic CD case, studies the song list on the back. "But I skip a couple that are boring: tracks 3, 4, 9, 13 . . . I listen to it in my car, with the windows down, you know . . ."

I say nothing. I'm dying to talk about the album, about the decided shift to pop that it represents in Céline's English-language career . . . This woman has just nonchalantly demonstrated a certain interest in my idol, but it's not enough yet. Not safe enough. Too many risks, still.

She cannot possibly understand the war playing out in my head. She opens the case, struggles to take out the CD, and says very loudly, "Do you mind if I put this on instead? Personally, I can't take any more Enya. It's the same thing in Lévis."

"I Drove All Night" blares out in the shop. It blows me away to hear Céline's voice among the wooden ducks and scented candles. That would never have happened under Manon Sirois. The temporary manager massacres a few lyrics, clicks her nails on the counter in time to the bass. Then she moves to the display case where the fake Heart of the Ocean sparkles and points at it wordlessly. I imagine she wants to emphasize the connection between the music playing in the store and the necklace.

"The song from *Titanic*! The same singer," she explains.

I smile inanely. She moves back over to the cash.

"We have one in Lévis, too. I don't understand what we're doing with it. No one would ever buy it."

I'm forced to agree with her.

When the second song starts, Linda's attention wanders. Not such a big fan, apparently. "I'm going out for a smoke."

She abandons me in the knick-knack store, alone with myself and the speakers playing "Love Is All We Need," a daring song about conjugal violence. I'm floating outside my body—that's the effect that hearing Céline Dion in a public place has on me: the sensation of sharing something with people, of feeling my existence validated, even if the people around me couldn't care less about the music, probably aren't even listening to it.

The bell above the door jingles. It's an older woman in a dark purple skirt—our typical customer. She very slowly peruses the displays. Caresses a stuffed animal, strokes a knick-knack, lifts it up to check the price, puts it back down . . . She dilly-dallies so much that by the time she approaches the cash, track 7, "Naked," is playing. A country pop gem with a dazzling change of octave. I don't understand why it hasn't been released as a single. The customer smiles at me.

"They've changed the music here," she says. "Usually, they have fiddlers playing."

This woman is out to lunch. She must be confusing us with the Christmas shop. Our background music is always New Age. I smile back at her faintly.

"Who sings this?" she asks.

I can't believe she doesn't recognize the voice. I struggle to control myself. "I *think* it's Céline Dion."

A look of contempt. "Not crazy about her. I prefer Laurence Jalbert."

Oh, the audacity! I shut my mouth; I have nothing to say to that. The lady must think I've lost my manners because soon after, she leaves the store without so much as a goodbye.

21

OFF HER ROCKER

AS SOON AS I TELL MY FATHER that Manon Sirois is on sick leave, he launches into a story about how he ran into her three weeks ago on rue du Campanile, pushing an old lady in a wheelchair.

"It looked like it was her mother or an aunt . . . In any case, I passed them and I wanted to say hello, but forget about it. She was looking at the sidewalk. I never managed to catch her eye. Really bizarre. I ended up practically kneeling down so she'd look at me. Nothing. But she's seen me before; she knows I'm her employee's father. Eh, Colin? She's seen me before. I dropped you off at work once . . ."

My mother doesn't think it's serious. "Sometimes women don't feel like speaking to men who make faces at them on the sidewalk, Daniel. Maybe her mind was elsewhere. Maybe she was concentrating on not bumping into the wheelchair. The few times I've seen her, I found her nice. Eh, Colin?"

"She's nuts," I say simply.

My mother rolls her eyes. “Well, honestly, what makes her nuts?”

“She makes me relabel all the junk in the store on Sundays so she can sit on her butt the rest of the week.”

“That’s why you call her nuts?”

I think about it. “Yes. Plus, she calls me ‘beautiful’ all the time.”

“She must be off her rocker if she calls you that,” Clément quips.

He and Catherine Moreau burst out laughing. Their bond seems to be largely built on the bitchy remarks my brother directs at me. In any case, his ultra-polite girlfriend seems to have loosened up pretty quickly.

Because, yes, Miss Future Doctor is back at our table this evening. I hope it doesn’t become a habit; it would be nice to have the weekends off. And I’d really like to be able to sit at my own spot from time to time. Catherine Moreau may well intend to have a phenomenal career, but she’s not really part of our family.

My father continues his little investigation. “Do your parents live together, Catherine?”

“No, they’ve been separated for seven years,” she replies. “I live with my mother and her boyfriend, my brother and our stepsister.”

I add, for my parents’ benefit, “Her stepsister is Catherine Crosnier, you know, the girl who fainted in my class the other day." I refrain from adding that she's also the biggest fake in the school.

"Oh yes, her!" my mother says. "She's recovered from her little episode, I hope."

Catherine Moreau nods. She's busy swallowing big spoonfuls of soup. She sounds like a sink draining, but my brother says nothing. Love is changing him, little by little.

I am officially the only single person in the Bourque family. Life is denying me happiness, a romance with my brother's girlfriend's brother.

22

LEATHER STRAPS

IT'S FRIDAY. Returning from school, Eugénie and I get off the number 7 in front of the video store. The plan: dinner at my best friend's and movie night.

We linger for a long time in the aisles, reading the backs of the boxes, going back and forth a lot . . . Eugénie wants to watch *Spice World* again, but honestly, I don't have fond memories of that movie. I'd rather rent *Catch Me If You Can*: Leonardo DiCaprio looks amazing in it.

Finally, in a strange turn of events, we leave the video store with *Twister*. Apparently the compromise between *Spice World* and *Catch Me If You Can* is a movie about tornadoes.

We arrive at Eugénie's just as her father is walking down the hallway in his white briefs. He bursts out laughing and retraces his steps, apologizing. My friend looks at me out of the corner of her eye as if my reaction will determine hers. Embarrassed, I grin foolishly before hanging up my coat and heading toward the bathroom. As I pass Eugénie's parents' room, I venture a sideways glance. Michel, bare-chested, is zipping up his pants. The scene is disturbingly arousing.

: :

Eugénie's mother has made a huge pot of macaroni and cheese and a veggie platter. It's simple and delicious. At home, we never eat raw vegetables unless it's a child's birthday. Sitting at the head of the table, Michel proclaims, "Enjoy!"

My friend's father has a deep voice. He's tall, bearded—rather attractive for an older man. I had never really noticed him before today. The love I have for Yann Moreau is opening my eyes to a great many things, like the virile beauty of Eugénie's father.

Liette observes me in silence. After my first bite, she rushes to ask, "Is it too hot?"

I shake my head. She disappears for a moment and returns with the salt and pepper shakers. "Don't be shy to add salt, I won't be insulted. I didn't know if you prefer your food salty or . . ."

My best friend's mother is the type of woman who always thinks about others and never herself. She'd be the perfect candidate for one of those home renovation shows where they redecorate the bedrooms of selfless women who put other people's needs ahead of their own.

Here, everyone is always smiling. But I have to admit, when Eugénie comes to my place, my parents also make an effort to be friendly. Having dinner guests forces people to be in a good mood.

"Are your parents well, Colin?" Michel asks.

Are my parents well? Are my parents poorly? My parents are a fact of life; they exist and I exist alongside them without being overly aware of their condition.

"Yes, I think so."

Michel, Liette and Eugénie look at one another, laughing.

"What? What's so funny?"

They keep laughing. They can't stop. Their humour is infectious, and I join in the hilarity.

When things finally calm down, Eugénie's mother says, "It was the way you said it . . ."

And that sets them off again, and me with them. I take the opportunity to contemplate Michel, his thin lips fringed with the brown hair of his beard, his thick eyebrows. I think about his work in finance, at Desjardins, and it makes him seem even more mature to me, stronger, reassuring. In mere moments, I have become a pervert who fantasizes about his best friend's father. It's crazy how quickly things change.

: :

Twister is over the top. At the end, Helen Hunt ties herself to a pipe with leather straps so she won't fly away when the tornado passes overhead. Ridiculous!

Before leaving, I ask Eugénie if she has ever caught her parents making love. Her eyes practically bug out of her head. "No! You?" she cries.

"Me neither."

Walking home, I cringe at myself for even asking the question.

23

A SANDPAPER FACTORY

MY MOTHER HAS TWO WOMEN FRIENDS she almost never sees. That's what happens when you're an adult: you no longer really have any friends; you have only your family. I've had only Eugénie forever, so I'm already living the life of an adult.

One of my mother's two friends is called Ghislaine Baril, and she came into the world on the fifteenth of November. This year, it falls on a Saturday, and my mother has decided to bring her a gift and catch up. I'm going with her because Eugénie isn't available to see me today. And I really like going places with Marie-Louise.

My father and Clément have gone off to a swim meet. I would have preferred to go with them—one hundred times over—to see Yann Moreau in a Speedo, but it would have been far too suspicious. I've never shown the slightest interest in my brother's sport. If I want to see Yann Moreau again, I'd better find another way. Time is passing; the weeks have flown by since the party, and I'm feeling more and more alone in the world with my romantic feelings. Yann Moreau wouldn't even recognize me if he ran into me on the street. He's forgotten the whole encounter.

My mother's friend lives in a village in the Beauce region. From Sainte-Foy, it's more than an hour by car. We leave around ten o'clock to arrive at Ghislaine's before lunch. The weather is unusually nice and warm.

I chose some CDs for the car trip. Of course, there's Marie Carmen, but also Patricia Kaas, Loreena McKennitt and music from the Cirque du Soleil. I even slid a Céline Dion into the lot—*D'eux*, her only album that everyone seems to agree on.

I've only gone to Ghislaine Baril's place twice. She and my mother have been friends since childhood. When they were little, they were neighbours. But they drifted apart when my mother started university. Ghislaine married young and moved to Beauce with her husband. They have two children, twin girls my brother's age. Ghislaine works in a sandpaper factory. Her husband does odd jobs. At least that's what my father says.

"Ghislaine's husband does odd jobs here and there. He's never managed to hold down a job. He has a problem with authority."

I find it a bit stressful meeting new people. Since it's been at least five years since I last saw Ghislaine and her family, I consider them new people.

: :

My mother's friend is sitting in an old people swing in the middle of her yard. She sees our car and waves at us energetically. But there are a bunch of people milling around her, at least ten. I start to panic.

"What's going on?" I ask my mother.

"What do you mean, what's going on? We're here."

"Why are there so many people?"

"I don't know. They must be extended family, friends . . ."

"You didn't tell me there'd be so many people here."

My mother stares at me so completely blankly that I almost start sobbing. "I didn't know either, Colin. She invited people over."

My heart is racing. This is a disaster. To think I could have stayed quietly in Sainte-Foy. To think I chose to experience this.

"I thought we were going to see your friend and her family. You never said there'd be other people."

Marie-Louise thinks I'm complicated. She's beginning to lose patience. "Colin, it's her birthday."

I consider my options. Has anyone seen me? I could hide in the back seat and stay there all day. Or leave on the sly and roam the streets of the village, waiting for my mother.

Discouraged, I whine, "It's not cool to invite people over without telling them there are going to be other guests. It's super rude."

My mother opens her door.

"Wait!" I cry.

She turns back to me and hisses, "Enough. Come on."

: :

We've been at Ghislaine Baril's for an hour now, and I still haven't managed to tear myself away from my mother. I know I seem like a baby, but my fear is visceral. I wouldn't be able to face all these strangers without her by my side.

But eventually she has to go to the bathroom. I'm about to follow her, but she stops me. "Colin, really," she whispers. "Stay here. What's the matter with you?"

She doesn't wait for an answer. It's just a criticism disguised as a question. I don't want to embarrass her. But I feel unsafe here, with all these people, without her. I can't help it. It's beyond me, and I don't even know where it's coming from.

Everyone has moved to the kitchen, where Ghislaine is filling bowls of chips and taking out platters of sandwiches from the fridge. Her two daughters, the twins, are helping her. Her husband is sitting at the table with four other men. They are laughing loudly, drinking beer and digging into the bowls of chips. I don't want to talk to them.

I approach Ghislaine and act like I'm moving things around on the counter. I feel that's what I should be doing.

"So, d'you talk much?" one of the twins teases.

My cheeks blaze. I smile, nodding. How do I answer that? I speak when I want to. That's the kind of platitude people have been saying to me forever. It makes me want to be even more quiet, which doesn't help matters.

One of the twins is heavier than the other. She caresses her stomach while talking to her mother. She catches me looking at her belly.

"It's not fat, it's a mini-me."

My eyes widen. I don't really know what to say. "Oh!"

I'm pretty sure pregnant women typically expect to be congratulated on their pregnancies. Unfortunately, I didn't react the right way. But only because I'm paralyzed with fear by the general situation. I don't say anything else. She ignores me and switches to a baby voice, head lowered toward her own belly. "It's Mommy's wittle peanut!"

: :

The drive home has the effect of a mega dose of tranquilizers on me. I deflate slowly like a basketball, all my tension releasing. The day has exhausted me. I bitterly regret having come, but it's over. Marie-Louise probes in vain for confirmation that her sixteen-year-old son is not completely useless and unhinged. "Well, it wasn't that bad in the end, eh?"

I prefer to change the subject. "One of the twins is pregnant."

My mother remains impassive. "Yes, I know."

"But Mom! Ghislaine Baril's daughters are Clément's age."

"I know."

I gesticulate to make my point. "She's going to have a baby and she's eighteen! She's ruining her life. She's going to have to quit school!"

"I think she's already shit. Quit, I mean! Quit! I think she's already quit school. She wants to move in with the baby's father, but it's a bit complicated because he's older and already has a child. But it's her life, Colin. Just because it's not like yours doesn't mean you should judge her."

Marie-Louise finds it just as distressing as I do, I'd bet my life on it. I don't get why she's pretending to take the high ground. She loses it whenever she sees a pregnant teenager in a soap opera.

"You shouldn't be such a snob about it," she concludes.

Snob? Me? It's my mother who's a fake.

24

NAIL JEWELLERY

ON THE TIPS OF LINDA BEAUDOIN'S FAKE NAILS, there are little holes with charms attached. Her nails are bejewelled. Nail jewellery. The first time I noticed them, I died. I told Eugénie about it, and she went nuts, too. I didn't tell my mother, who would certainly call me a snob.

Manon Sirois still hasn't returned to the knick-knack shop.

25

EVERYONE IS FAKE

ON MONDAY, Ms. Parker tells us about our English project for the end of term: inventing a city. We have to find a name for our city, determine its geographic and demographic characteristics, draw a map . . . The work is divided into two parts: a poster and an oral presentation. It sounds a lot like something we did in Grade 9, but maybe it's hard to come up with original ideas for projects when you're an English teacher.

For this project, we'll have to form teams of two. Of course, Eugénie and I *always* team up; it's just a given. But Eugénie is absent this morning; she has a stomach bug. That doesn't change anything: I'll tell her about it when she gets back, and we'll work together.

That's definitely what I would do in normal circumstances.

But an idea has just taken hold in my mind. An idea that concerns Yann Moreau; an idea that could change the course of my life. It's a brilliant plan, I think, but I don't know if I dare execute it. Ms. Parker hasn't even finished explaining the project and already heads are turning; students are gesturing to one another and silently forging alliances. My cheeks redden and sweat drips down my back because I only have a few seconds to make my decision. A critical decision.

In a trance, almost outside my body, I turn around in my chair and look at the girl seated behind me, manage to catch her eye. I flash her a forced smile and whisper hysterically, "Want to work together?"

She looks surprised. I'm dying of embarrassment. I'm not acting normally—it's painful to watch. Colin Bourque *always* teams up with Eugénie Bujold.

But my neighbour gives me a joyful smile and nods her head.

And it's done. I'm paired up with Catherine Crosnier, Yann Moreau's stepsister. I have butterflies in my stomach. I've betrayed my best friend, but it's the only way I could think of to see my secret love again.

It's official: everyone is fake. Even me. Especially me.

26
YOU SUCK

“YOU TEAMED UP with *who*?”

Eugénie can’t believe it, and I get it. Aside from the fact that it’s the first time in five years I haven’t picked her as a teammate, I’ve set my sights on a girl I almost openly despise. But I can’t explain my choice to her: I’d have to tell her everything, everything . . . And I’m really not there yet.

“With Catherine Crosnier. You were away, Eug!”

“Well, yes, but I have to do the project, too! You knew I’d come back to school one day or another, all you had to do was wait. You suck, Colin!”

She’s reacting even worse than I’d thought. Yet Eugénie is a very sociable person; sometimes I wonder if she wants to hang out with other people, and I feel guilty thinking that I’m keeping her a prisoner, preventing her from being friends with whomever she wants. But now she’s disappointed. I trot out my last remaining lie.

“Honestly, she kind of asked me. It was sad, Eug . . . You know, Catherine Crosnier isn’t exactly the most popular girl in town. She could have ended up with Catherine Julien."

My friend grimaces. "Now I'm the one who'll end up with Catherine Julien!"

I'm sure I'm beet red. What have I done? This is the first time in ten years of friendship that Eugénie and I have had an argument. I'm not about to lose my best and only friend over a guy who might never be interested in me.

"I'm sorry, Eug. You're right, it wasn't cool of me. I'll tell Catherine Crosnier to find another partner."

"No, don't bother! I'll seem possessive. It's okay! I'll just have to work with Catherine Julien. But I don't understand why you didn't wait for me."

I'm relieved. My plan worked. Eugénie will get over it. She's a doll.

The butterflies return at the mere thought of seeing Yann Moreau, of being at Yann Moreau's house. In Yann Moreau's room.

Good lord, I have to calm down.

27

BLUE FUZZY BATHROBE

TODAY, SATURDAY, November 22, 2003, my life is going to change.

Here's something I didn't know about Catherine Crosnier: she's studious. Over-the-top studious. The English project is due on December 19, but madame has decided we have to start it immediately. On a Saturday morning. In normal circumstances, I would have invented a reason to get out of it, but since I've been sleeping terribly for weeks because I'm obsessed with her magnificent stepbrother, Catherine Crosnier's zealousness suits me just fine.

The Crosnier-Moreaus live in a mansion near school, on Marie-Victorin. In my neighbourhood full of bungalows, the few houses with two floors are considered manors. Here, that's all there is. This family has done well for themselves.

::

Damn. Catherine Crosnier has just informed me that her stepbrother is at a swim meet all day. She said it in passing, as if my universe hadn't just crumbled. She had the nerve to add, "Didn't you know your brother had a meet today? My stepsister went with them. Those things are so boring. Plus, we have too much work for that."

Well, damn. Clément, his Catherine Moreau of a girlfriend, and my Yann are spending the day together at a sports complex that smells like chlorine and testosterone. I should be there, too. Cheering on my secret love. I'm so blinded by disappointment that I can barely appreciate the super trendy decor of the house. There are granite counters in the kitchen and an in-ground pool in the backyard. If I weren't so depressed, I'd be swooning over every detail. But I sit down silently at the dining room table, across from my new fake friend who bores me more than ever.

The afternoon drags on. Paul Crosnier, my partner's father, is reading his newspaper in the living room, watching golf on TV. It's his girlfriend—Yann and Catherine Moreau's mother—who's gone to watch the swim meet.

Catherine Crosnier and I are making rather good progress. She's thought a lot about the English project. Her ideas don't wow me, but they're reasonable enough and should earn us a good grade. We decide to call our city Theatre City because it will be filled with amazing cultural attractions. Catherine starts designing the map of Theatre City. She draws decently. The work is less tedious than I'd imagined, and I relax enough to ask, "Do you get along well with your stepbrother?"

She doesn't look up from the construction paper. "Yann? Fine."

Brief silence.

"He's the rebel of the family," she continues.

Rebel! The word surprises me, but I accept it. I'm prepared to take Yann as he is. Details, please.

"A rebel—how?"

She puts down her pencil and sighs. "He'd like to do away with the capitalist system."

She says this in a superior tone. I'm not sure I know what the capitalist system is, but I think it's the world we live in: it's life, reality, the Quebec of 2003; it's nice houses and in-ground pools. I don't understand why you'd want to do away with the outcome of human evolution. I'm both frightened by this plan and attracted by the complexity of Yann Moreau, by the depth of his soul. Basically, I know nothing. Having good grades in high school doesn't mean you understand anything.

::

It's after five o'clock and I'm fed up with Theatre City. Usually, with Eugénie, we do things at the last minute. Now, a month before the due date, the project is already half-finished. Catherine Crosnier is gung-ho like you wouldn't believe.

The front door opens, and into the dining room spill my brother, Clément; his girlfriend; and Yann Moreau. Yann looks surprised to see me sitting with his stepsister.

"Hey! Hi, you two!" he says quickly.

"Hey!" Catherine Crosnier replies, still drawing.

"Hey! Hi, you three!" I blurt out, a volcano erupting in my stomach, sweating with emotion.

I just copied his answer but changed the number, which is idiotic.

I've only seen Yann twice, so I've never been able to observe him up close. His brown hair is tousled like my brother's—swimmer's hair. For the first time, I find that attractive. His little black eyes shine with intelligence. He's no taller than me, but I'm sure that next to him, I must look like a child. Now I can confirm it; it's official, definite: Yann Moreau is the hottest guy I've ever seen.

The mother, who walked in right after her children, stands in front of me.

"You must be Colin Bourque, Clément's brother. I'm Denise. Delighted."

She holds out a hand with cherry-red nails that I am forced to shake despite my extremely sweaty palms—a detail that Denise Moreau deems relevant to share with everyone.

"Your hands are all moist, dear! I hope I'm not making you nervous!"

Her strange, halting laughter hits me in the face. Catherine Crosnier, Catherine Moreau and Clément stare at me like the circus animal I feel myself becoming. Yann looks uncomfortable. Awful! My body is betraying my feelings; my body doesn't know how to lie. I'm going to die of shame.

"Will you stay and have dinner with us, Colin?" Denise adds. "I'm going to order in chicken."

Reluctantly, I accept. I refuse to give up this chance—perhaps my only chance—of getting closer to my secret love. Even if his mother finds me moist and insignificant.

: :

The meal is chaotic, with Clément and Yann trying to talk about their day, Denise interrupting them every two seconds to provide unimportant details, and Paul Crosnier trying to make his daughter laugh by pestering her when she just wants to eat her nuggets in peace (the man seems hungry for attention).

After dinner, I find myself in a sort of social vortex. I'm not really anyone's friend (Catherine Crosnier invited me over, but it was for the English project, and now she's gone upstairs to take a bath, which is unsettling). My brother couldn't give a damn about me (he and his girlfriend are shut up in a bedroom listening to music), and Yann Moreau has withdrawn to the basement. Paul and

Denise are watching an action movie on TV. I can't believe I'm going to spend my Saturday night with them, huddled in a corner, trying to disappear until someone offers to drive me home. Where is my life headed?

But it's my only option. I slip into the living room and sit down as quietly as possible in a leather armchair that squeaks at my slightest movement.

"Shush!" whispers the mother, giving me a wink. This joker stresses me out more than the threat of terrorism.

The lame movie unfolds without anyone paying me the slightest bit of attention. It must be nine o'clock. At one point, Catherine Crosnier enters the living room in a blue fuzzy bathrobe and, without the slightest glance my way, sits down next to her father on the sofa. Am I supposed to go outside and wait for the bus without saying a word?

28

CALLIN' COLIN

THE VILLAIN OF THE MOVIE has just been shot in the shoulder, and I'm on the verge of begging Mr. Crosnier for a lift home when, out of nowhere, Yann Moreau appears.

"Mom, Cat? You know it really sucks that you're forcing Colin to watch your dumb movie?"

How well he understands me. For form's sake, I protest weakly. "It's okay . . ."

Denise shamelessly eyes me up and down. "Well, we can't read his mind, eh, Colin?"

Marie-Louise would find this lady quite rude. How different my secret love's parents are from mine!

Caught off guard, I repeat, "It's okay . . ."

Yann signals me to join him. I get up, but no one seems to care; so much the better. He leads me to the basement.

"Sorry, what a boring evening for you!"

I still can't come up with anything else to say—shit!—except for this annoying phrase: "It's okay . . ."

Yann Moreau laughs. “It’s fine, I get it. You don’t have to be polite with me. I know my family is weird.”

And before I realize what’s happening, he opens a door and ushers me into a room. *His room*. Paradise.

::

For half an hour I’ve been sitting on Yann Moreau’s desk chair. For half an hour he’s been lying on his bed. For half an hour time has stood still. We talk about school, Clément, college, our families. Everything is going well. When Yann is talking, I’m free to study his face, to engrave it on my memory. I like everything about him. Even the pimple sprouting next to his nostril.

The conversation slows and silence settles in. I slide my hands under my butt. Yann straightens up on his bed, moves toward the edge of the mattress, toward me. He smiles at me, but he smiles all the time, so it means absolutely nothing. He smiles because he is Jack Dawson in *Titanic*. If I were Jack, I would smile all the time, too, except for at the end of the movie.

I’m about ready to explode like a bag of popcorn, and two lakes have formed under my armpits.

“Do you really want to do away with the entire capitalist system?” I blurt without thinking.

Yann Moreau bursts out laughing. "Did my stepsister tell you that?"

I laugh softly, screwing up my eyes. Yann plunges his gaze into mine and says, "Actually, I want to overthrow the rich."

Silence. His brown eyes rattle me so badly that it takes some time for me to register his answer. I finally say, "Overthrow the rich? But *you are* rich."

"My *parents* are rich. I don't have a cent."

"Well, yeah, but it's the same thing. You benefit from it all the same. You live in a mansion."

His beautiful laugh again. "Let's just say it's not my ultimate aim in life. I'm not going to get rich doing film studies . . ."

"What do your parents do?"

"My mother is a lawyer, and my stepfather is an actuary."

My gosh. More prestigious careers. Yann is the only member of this family destined for the life of a penniless artist.

"What do yours do?" he asks.

"They work for the government," I say distastefully.

He laughs again. "You say that like you're telling me your parents are in prison for murder."

"It's practically worse!"

Yann finds me very funny, I can tell. I feel in control. He turns toward his stereo system.

"I could put on some music. What do you like?"

Oh no, not this. I'm sick of lying, but telling the truth is out of the question, not here, not this evening, not for ages, not before we're married. I reply with a stock answer. "A bit of everything!"

I'm sure he finds that fake, but he doesn't show it. "I'll put on Nelly Furtado."

His stereo plays "I'm Like a Bird," a song everyone likes. Yann Moreau motions to me. "Come sit on the bed! You'll be more comfortable."

Trembling like a leaf, I lie down next to him on his big mattress. My arm brushes his; it would take only a tiny gesture to hold his hand, caress his thigh, curl up against his neck. Immobile, I revel in being there, so close to him, without really touching him, savouring the air he breathes. The fruity smell of his shampoo sends me into the stratosphere.

::

Back at home, I have a premonition. I turn on the computer in secret and open MSN. Yann Moreau has added me to his contacts. He must have got my address from his stepsister. His nickname is just as cool as he is: Yannolito—Be ThE cHaNgE yOu WaNt To SeE iN tHe WoRlD. Mine is pathetic next to it: Callin' Colin. In my defence, it was Eugénie who came up with it.

As soon as I connect, he sends me a little message:

It was cool seeing you this evening!
Sleep well! Sweet dreams! :)

I can't stop smiling. I have just won the lottery.

29

YO

MY LIFE HAS CHANGED. I now have only one plan in mind: to seduce Yann Moreau. Only one desire: to chat with him on MSN.

But I'm babbling, I'm talking nonsense: "to seduce Yann Moreau," as if I could, as if I had the slightest idea of what that means. The guy is in his second year of college, wants to study film in Montreal next year, swims, plans to do away with the entire capitalist system, and has the stunning physique of a fictional character who froze to death clinging to a door in the North Atlantic.

This morning, I undressed and examined myself in front of the bathroom mirror. What do I look like? I find nothing attractive about myself. I should have played more sports in high school. I would have developed differently; I'd be a little straighter, broader, less ordinary. I'd have better posture and arms that fill out the sleeves of a shirt. Physical activity generally makes people desirable. Of course, there are exceptions: Guillaume

Brassard, the hot guy from Group B, isn't on any sports teams, but he hit the genetic jackpot.

It's sad and pathetic, but I'm going to have to rely on my personality to find my way through the world to Yann Moreau. Because my body doesn't look like much.

: :

For a week now I've been monopolizing the basement computer to chat with Yann. If he's not signed in, I wait; I kill time; I talk to Eugénie. As soon as his little man icon goes from red to green, a fever takes hold of me. I straighten up in my chair; my body trembles and overheats. Basically, I come alive. I'm alive: this is life. And all this time, I thought it was going to school during the week and to Eugénie's on weekends. But life is hoping for a message from Yann Moreau on MSN.

Most of the time, I have trouble controlling myself and start a conversation with him after a few seconds. Sometimes, I manage to talk myself down, and I wait. I wait for several long minutes. I imagine he's also just sitting there, waiting for me to make the first move. I play hard to get. I need him to come to me.

And he ends up giving in with a nonchalance that makes my heart leap:

Yo :)

Each time, it's a victory. I melt in front of the computer. Yann Moreau wants to talk to me. I didn't force his hand: he came willingly. I am the king of Sainte-Foy.

30

INDIFFERENCE

THIS SUNDAY, it's freezing cold, and my mother didn't offer me a lift to the knick-knack store. I'm shivering in the back of the number 7. I should have worn a hat and mittens, but then I'd look like a little kid, which is no longer acceptable now that I'm in love with an eighteen-year-old man.

When I get to the store, I notice that the door is unlocked and the lights are on. A woman who is neither Manon Sirois nor Linda Beaudoin is standing behind the counter. Tall, built like a truck and wearing a brown suit, she introduces herself, extending her hand.

"Hello, Colin. We've never met, but it's a pleasure. I'm Claudette Hallé. I'm the owner of the shop."

I mumble a lukewarm "hi, hi"; I don't understand what's going on and didn't expect to meet someone so high up this morning. Had I known, I would have fixed my hair differently. Claudette Hallé motions me to sit down on my stool.

"Do you know why I'm here?" she asks.

I have no idea, but I'm beginning to worry. Has someone exposed my misuse of MSN during work hours? Who? Linda Beaudoin? She isn't the type. Manon Sirois? Absent for weeks now. My cheeks blaze.

"Is Linda Beaudoin sick?" I ask innocently.

The owner places her index finger on her chin. "No, but that would be a very plausible reason, actually. Good thinking."

She's speaking to me like I'm a baby. Her gentle voice melds with the background music in the shop. "No, it's because something's happened to Manon Sirois."

Oh! That. "I know. She fell on the stairs," I say.

Claudette Hallé adopts a solemn expression. "That's true, Colin. You're right. But something else happened to her, at the hospital. She had to have surgery for her injuries, last week, and what happened . . . what happened is that . . . well, you see . . . during the operation, you know . . . it's because . . . it didn't go well."

And?

"Unfortunately, Manon died. I'm really sorry."

I fall into a tunnel. The walls of the shop distort around me. The neon lights turn into strobe lights, and the air gets very thin. As I feel myself falling backward, I grab onto the edge of the seat. Claudette Hallé takes a leap forward and grabs me by the shoulders. "Are you okay, Colin?"

I jerk away from her violently, without thinking. She backs up a few steps, observing me like I'm a pitiful puppy. Manon Sirois is dead. Manon Sirois, the person who made me relabel all the Pierrot dolls and puppets. She is deceased. At this very moment, she is no more than a heap of inert cells, a stiff corpse that air and time will end up putrefying.

I hear myself asking a series of mundane questions. "How old was she?"

"She was fifty-three."

"Did she have children?"

"No. She lived with her mother."

"Will Linda Beaudoin be the new manager?"

"I don't know yet. But you don't have to worry about that, Colin."

"Are we going to open the shop today?"

Claudette Hallé places her hand on the glass counter, very close to me.

"It's up to you, Colin. If you don't feel like working, I'll understand and you can go home. It's not exactly a normal day, eh?"

I nod my head, eyes glued to the floor. What am I supposed to feel? I am not—or don't think I am—sad or distressed. Stunned, more like it. Flabbergasted. Unnerved. I was expecting a Sunday like any other, and now I have to deal with the death of my boss, meet her boss, decide my own fate, make a choice . . . I know my reaction isn't the right one, that someone else would shed a tear or two, would rather go home, spend time with his family, be visibly shaken. Instead, I say, "If I stay, will I be paid?"

Claudette Hallé looks surprised. She is silent for a few seconds, like she's waiting to see if I'm going to add anything else. Finally, she replies, "Yes, Colin. Don't worry. If you stay, you'll be paid."

So I settle in behind the computer, like every other Sunday, to sell knick-knacks to the old people in the neighbourhood. That's what Manon Sirois would have wanted.

::

My parents flip out.

At dinner, as soon as I tell them my boss died, my mother starts giving me sorrowful looks and my father rubs my back. Even Clément paints a strange grimace on his face. I try to tell them I'm fine, but they still treat me like a tearful child. They don't know me. I feel nothing, nothing, nothing at all. Feeling nothing is possible. Indifference exists. It isn't a problem; it's an emotion like any other. It means that Manon Sirois was nothing to me. That's all. Maybe it's stupid, but that's all.

::

After dinner, I connect to MSN, and Yann Moreau starts the conversation immediately:

Him: *Yo :)*
Me: *Hey!*
Him: *What's new?*
Me: *My boss died.*
Him: *Oh no! :(*
Me: *LOL*
Him: *But you're OK?*
Me: *Yes, I didn't like her. Well, I didn't want her to die, but like, I didn't care. LOL*
Him: *Sorry all the same :(*
Me: *Thanks. That's nice of you.*

I don't know what else to say to him. Our usual bond has been cooled by Manon Sirois' demise. I picture her calling me "beautiful" as she tosses her purse down on the counter, and tears spring to my eyes. I don't understand why, and I wipe them away angrily. After a moment, Yann Moreau writes:

Want to talk about it in person?

Through my tears, a smile:

YES!

So he doesn't think I'm too intense, I quickly offer an excuse:

Me: *Sorry, I hit Caps Lock. LOL.*
Him: *Ha. I'll borrow my mother's car and meet you in 15 minutes?*
Me: *Yesss: D*

Thank you, Manon.

31
SORROW

SURPRISINGLY FOR A SUNDAY EVENING, my parents immediately agreed to let me leave the house. I said I was going over to Eugénie's to watch TV. They looked at each other, and my father murmured, "It's no ordinary day, eh, son? It'll do you good to see your friend."

Now he's talking exactly like Claudette Hallé; their compassion is annoying! I told them I was fine.

"As long as you're home by ten o'clock," Marie-Louise adds. "You have school tomorrow."

I agree without protest. That gives me more than two hours alone in the city with Yann Moreau. Freedom.

::

I asked Yann Moreau to meet me in the video store parking lot so my parents don't see me getting into a strange car. The wind bites at my face and fingers, but I could wait hours for him. When he finally arrives, it's behind the wheel of his mother's black BMW. Incredibly classy.

I get in next to him, euphoric, and immediately ask what excuse he gave his parents for meeting me. He looks at me, puzzled. "I told them the truth, that I was spending the evening with a friend."

A blunder. For him, there's nothing compromising, nothing questionable about this situation. He sees me as just a friend, or worse, as the little brother of one of his friends. Not to mention, he's eighteen and clearly does what he wants. I'm such a loser!

"Why do you ask? What did you tell your parents?"

My cheeks, already chapped, turn a little more crimson. I decide to make the best of the situation. "That I was going out to meet an old pedophile in the video store parking lot."

Then I burst out in uncontrollable laughter. After chuckling politely, Yann Moreau says, "But really, you didn't tell them the truth?"

Will he just let it go? I should have shut my mouth, as usual; now I'm stuck in a stupid situation caused by my romantic ecstasy. Either I continue cracking jokes about it—after all, maybe he likes guys with a sense of humour—or I lie and say that I told my parents the truth, or I tell the truth and admit that I lied to them. The decision is made on its own, with no effort: I lie.

"No, no, I'm joking. I told them I was going out with you."

An awkward turn of phrase. I backpedal. “Well, you know what I mean . . . In the sense of ‘leaving the house.’ I told them I was going to see you, not that I was going out with you.”

I detect a mischievous smile behind his scarf. A shiver of ecstasy. Imagine if he likes me the way I like him?

::

Yann Moreau parks the BMW on rue Mont-Carmel, very close to the Château Frontenac. Then we walk over to terrasse Dufferin. Old Quebec is deserted; the snow is gently falling, and I feel like I’m in a scene from a Hollywood movie. If I held out my arm to him, just a bit, if I stretched out my fingers . . . I quiver just thinking about it.

He breaks the silence. “So, your boss . . .”

My gosh, I’d forgotten about that. My happiness at being here, with him, is overshadowing everything else. I dig deep within myself the way I search through my locker at school; where have I stashed my sadness? Slow to emerge at first, it now seems to have been completely absorbed; I’ve absorbed it all.

“Why didn’t you like her?” Yann continues.

I take a deep breath, searching for an answer that is both sincere and empathetic. “You know . . . She was my boss. She bossed me around.”

“Oh . . .”

He seems to find that lame. I clear my throat. "No, but . . . She didn't want me to go on MSN during work hours."

That is the honest truth. Too bad if he judges me; I'm fed up with lying. But he laughs.

"I know it sounds dumb," I say, "but when there's nothing to do . . . You can't imagine how boring it is at the knick-knack shop, on Sundays."

He laughs again. I liven up, put on a show for him, tell stories, describe the objects we sell, imitate the customers. Soon, he's doubled over with laughter. I'm proud; I feel taller, radiant. I'm almost brave enough to take his hand.

Yann catches his breath. "You make me laugh!"

Silence. The wind ruffles the already-tousled hair of my secret love. He's looking at me; I'm looking at the lights of Lévis.

"I'm really sorry that she died," he says.

Tears fill my eyes—it was there all along, my sorrow, lying in wait for me—I look up to hold them back.

I simply say, "Thanks very much, Yann."

::

At home, I get into bed with my Discman and listen to "Where Does My Heart Beat Now" fourteen times in a row; nothing else seems to match my emotions. I cry for a long time, hovering between elation and sorrow.

32

GRAND PALACE

CÉLINE'S FATHER HAS DIED. He was a strange man with a strange name and a strange face. The Dion family is not immortal. It's hard to believe, but even Céline will die, one day, confined to her bed in a grand palace filled with awards. But on that day and all the ones that follow, her voice will still remain.

Everyone is dying, these days.

33

COLD LUNCHES

CLAUDETTE HALLÉ SUGGESTS I approach the corpse. She urges me to pray for Manon Sirois. I don't want to see the body up close. I'm not given the choice. Even Eugénie pushes me forward gently.

There's a little step where you can kneel and act like you're gathering your thoughts. I lean my shin against it. The corner of the wood digs into my skin. I remain immobile for a full minute, concentrating on the sensation in my leg. The pain acts as a screen, and right behind it I see flickering images of a ridiculous memory: the time Manon Sirois watched me without my knowing it, called me into the back of the store and scolded me for "surfing the Web during work hours." Poor Manon. I made her life difficult.

A woman in a wheelchair who looks like the old lady in *Titanic* is shaking people's hands next to the body: the deceased's mother. Her face is ravaged, resigned, exhausted. She never thought she'd have to bury her daughter. I hear her tell someone that, in the end, the spot on her lung was nothing.

Nothing at all. To think that Manon, one month earlier, had been crying over the thought of losing her mother. It's a terrible scene, a scene that tears me to shreds.

But I have no intention of breaking down in front of all these people. I make a vague gesture with my arms, one that I imagine looks religious, and pull Eugénie toward the exit. "Let's get out of here."

"No way!" she says. "I'm hungry, and I have no intention of wasting my money at Ashton. I want party sandwiches and pasta salad."

A fan of cold lunches, Eugénie has come for the buffet—and because there was no way I was showing up here alone. I remind her that we still have to sit through the funeral service. In a real church, with hard pews, no food and no bathrooms. We won't be eating for at least two hours. Her stomach begins rumbling loud enough to awaken a dead store manager; we leave quickly.

: :

On the 800 bus, Eugénie tries to lead me to the back, where a gang of guys is talking loudly. I resist and tell her I want to stay standing; we're getting off in less than ten minutes. She doesn't care.

As we cross the Archambault parking lot, we're almost run over by a Ford Focus. It's my mother. The window is lowered. Eugénie plasters a huge smile on her face.

"Hello, Marie-Louise!"

I have a long face; my mother shouts, "Colin! Be careful in the parking lot. Walk next to Simons, like everyone else."

No one says anything, so she continues. "I found the CD your father wanted and I bought you some new undies. Are you going home after this? Eugénie, are you having dinner with us? I have to go to the grocery store, I can buy big sausages."

I want to slap my mother (imagine her mentioning my "undies"; I'm sure cool guys my age wear boxers). Eugénie says she'd enjoy that, she loves sausages. The Focus moves away toward boulevard Laurier.

"Your mother's so nice, Colin."

I frown. That's not unusual; I also find Eugénie's mother more interesting than my own.

::

Sitting in front of our poutines and chicken sandwiches, we swallow everything noisily, taking long sips of our soft drinks. The food court at Place Ste-Foy is smaller than the one at Place Laurier, but I prefer it. It's full of blonde ladies from Sillery; there are no crying children, and you're less likely to run into people from school. In any case, there are Ashton restaurants everywhere.

"How did you feel seeing your boss in a coffin?" Eugénie asks.

"It was nice," I reply morosely.

We giggle, but that's not what I really think. Truth be told, it was painful; I almost burst out sobbing. I feel empty. Where did my sorrow go?

The afternoon passes slowly. We wander between Simons, Laura Secord, Archambault, Holt Renfrew—where we're followed around like criminals—and Les Ailes de la Mode. Eugénie suggests we go over to Place Laurier, but I'm worn out. Shopping malls exhaust me, especially when I'm wearing a big winter coat. We flop down on a bench and rest our eyes on the terracotta tiles.

::

On the way home, on the bus, we find ourselves stuck in the middle of a pack of ladies laden down with bags. We waited too long to leave; the stores are closing. Plus, we missed the 13. We're on the 801, and we're going to have to walk almost fifteen minutes to get home—practically to the Serengeti. The bus lets us off at the corner of Quatre-Bourgeois and de la Colline. Already fed up, I sigh loudly, dragging my feet. Dusk is falling; the snow crunches beneath our boots. My best friend is humming No Doubt.

Walking down avenue de Cherbourg, we spot Guillaume Pinette in the distance, walking toward us—the tall blond guy who bullied me in Grade 6. Fortunately, I live halfway up the hill, and we dash into the house before passing him. I know Eugénie would have greeted him nicely; she lives on another planet.

: :

In the centre of the table, there's a huge platter of sausages; around it, the Bourque family—it's a miracle! My brother's girlfriend is eating at her own house—and Eugénie.

"Were there a lot of people at the funeral?" my father asks.

I mutter a "yes," my mouth full of rice. My mother slaps the table impatiently.

"Honestly, Daniel, they didn't go to the actual funeral, only to the visitation. I told you earlier."

She turns to my friend. "Were there a lot of people at the funeral parlour?"

Eugénie stifles a laugh. She adores Marie-Louise's sudden outbursts, her intransigence. Her mother is easygoing; she smiles while she curls her hair in the mirror and never raises her voice.

"Mom, I just told you there were," I say.

"Yes, but Daniel was talking about the funeral, not the parlour."

"But you just said we didn't go to the funeral; if I said yes, I must have been talking about the parlour, don't you think?"

She readjusts her blouse and falls silent, one eyebrow raised.

Clément begins an endless story about a tennis match he saw on TV at his friend Guillaume Trahan's house. My father asks him a stream of questions about another match, another athlete and even—heaven help us—another sport. It's obvious my mother couldn't care less. She shakes the salad bowl and offers Eugénie anything and everything: bread, butter, water, more rice, more salad dressing. The sports story ends after an eternity. Marie-Louise looks at my friend and says in a clear voice, "How are your parents, dear?"

Parents are never friends with other parents, but they always ask about them like they are. It gives them a topic of conversation.

34

RATTLING MY ORNAMENTS

CLÉMENT IS PLAYING LOUD MUSIC IN HIS ROOM. I can't make out what it is, but it's rattling my ornaments. I jump up on my bed. Eugénie turns on my stereo.

"Not too loud," I order.

"Come on, relax. Your brother doesn't seem to care."

"Yes, but my brother doesn't listen to Céline Dion."

She makes a face. "Your whole family knows you're crazy about her. They're not going to throw you out because we're listening to her in your room."

I roll my eyes. "You don't understand. You don't live with a judgmental family."

"Neither do you!" she declares.

Play. The sound springs forth, rich and enveloping: magnificent chords struck on the piano. Eugénie selected *Falling Into You*, her favourite album, which opens with her favourite song. I'm stressed. I watch the minutes tick by on the digital display of the stereo—it's an intense song, epic, and above all, never-ending. At exactly five minutes and five seconds, the beat in the next room stops abruptly. Céline's voice bounces off the walls, inundates the room, the entire house, spills over into the street. Eugénie shouts:

There were nights of endless pleasure
It was more than all your laws allow
Baby, baby, baby
When you touch me like this
And when you hold me like that
It was gone with the wind
But it's all coming back to me

Cold sweat gathers in my armpits. Clément bangs loudly three times on our shared wall.

"Turn down your godawful music!"

Nothing stops my best friend; she continues to sing over the CD. I rush to the volume dial like it's a valve holding back the floodwaters of the Saguenay River. The diva falls silent; my brother's bass starts up again.

Eugénie joins me on the bed.

"You can't live like this, it's ridiculous! You should stand up for yourself. You have the right to do what you want."

She's getting on my nerves. Besides, what is she still doing here? I only have one thing on my mind: Yann Moreau. The evening is going by, and

I haven't spoken to him in two days. I try a not-so-subtle tactic to get my friend to leave.

"Ugh! I have a big day at the knick-knack shop tomorrow!"

Exaggerated yawning. But it goes right over Eugénie's head. The first velvet notes of "Because You Loved Me" have barely rung out when she reaches over and skips the CD to "All by Myself," which she strikes up in unison with Céline. How ironic that all I'm dreaming of is a bit of solitude . . . I break out the big guns.

"Well! Eug, it's not that I want to throw you out, but . . ."

She interrupts herself, turns her stunned face toward me. "Are you kicking me out, Colin Bourque?"

"No!" I said. "It's not that I want to throw you out, but . . ."

Eugénie Bujold stares daggers at me. "Finish your sentence."

"Well . . . I'm falling asleep and I have to work tomorrow morning."

Her tone is icy. "Yeah, I see that. It's seven-thirty. I don't know what's been going on with you recently. You teamed up with a girl you can't stand, you almost never talk to me on MSN anymore, and now you're giving me the boot."

I shrug. "Doesn't a guy have the right to be tired?"

"It's something else. You never kick me out. In all our lives, you've never done that."

I look down, playing with my nails.

"Colin, are you blowing me off?"

"Come on, Eug!" I cry.

I know she's confused, that she's only trying to understand. But her furrowed brow and her frown frighten me; I interpret them—wrongly, I'm sure—as the disgust she's sure to feel about my reality, as a feeling of alarm that traps me in panic and silence. All I'd need to do, at this precise instant, to change my life, to no longer be alone, would be to answer her question. I know it. But I wall myself in.

With a violent movement, Eugénie cranks up the volume on the stereo to the max, picks up her bag and leaves my room without turning around. The door closes exactly on the bridge, the tormented cry, Céline's great feat:

All by myself
Don't wanna be
All by myself
Anymore

The house has cracked in two. Clément bangs against the wall in protest, but I no longer hear anything.

: :

The mattress squeaks; I toss and turn endlessly, thinking about the words buried deep inside me, the ones I couldn't share with Eugénie. And what I said at Place Ste-Foy: that Manon Sirois in her coffin "was nice." A few tears dampen my pillow. I love a man with my entire tiny soul, and I'm not even lovable myself.

35

SOAPY PUDDLE

A MIRACLE OCCURRED THIS SATURDAY: my brother vomited up his breakfast. My father swore because the vomit landed on the table, my mother flipped out, and I wiped up the mess with paper towel.

Clément dragged himself to the bathroom to finish puking. Then he shut himself in his room, where Dad went to see him. I heard them discussing things for a while, and when he returned to the kitchen, Daniel announced, "Well! He won't make it to his swim meet! Apparently, the gentleman drank too much last night with his buddies."

My father was annoyed. But Marie-Louise didn't really care. "He's eighteen. He's at that age. There are worse things in life, huh?"

My mother does not consider competitive sports to be important.

Daniel grumbled a little and the conversation fizzled out because there was nothing more to say. I rejoiced inwardly. An avenue had opened up.

: :

Sitting in the last row of the bleachers, I stare at the clear water of the Olympic-sized pool. There is no crowd, just small groups of family members and friends scattered here and there. I have not run into Yann Moreau's mother or sister.

In a few minutes, he will come out of the locker room or somewhere else—I don't know how all that works. He'll approach the pool, adjust his goggles and his bathing suit, his tiny swimsuit, and do what he does best. Yann Moreau is both Jack in *Titanic* and his antithesis, because the water will never kill him.

Here they come. An entire group of them appears, walking toward the pool. I have trouble recognizing my secret love. Oh, there he is! One of the leanest on the team. From where I sit, these boys don't look like much: slender figures in black Speedos. But just the sight of Yann Moreau's bare chest, muscular legs, square shoulders, sends waves of pleasure throughout my body.

I remain in a trance for the entire competition. I don't know who's winning, who's losing; I watch Yann. He dives, moves his arms and legs, slices through the water like a torpedo, emerges from the pool in one quick movement. My jaw hangs open. His every move impresses me.

::

The swim meet is over. I don't really understand what signalled the end of the event, but everyone stands up and heads toward the exit, so I do the same.

There's a burning feeling in my belly. I change direction. I roam the corridors of the sports complex until I find the door to the locker room. I walk in like I belong there. I don't even know what's happening. I've lost control.

Inside, it's warm and humid, and it smells of shampoo. The sound of the showers throws me into a panic. What am I doing here?

My steps lead me toward the boys' voices, echoing in the distance, toward the water spraying the floor tiles after having caressed their bodies. I am Céline in the video for "Ziggy," the nasty girl who spies on the athletes in the locker room.

Soon I find myself there, in the doorway of the shower room, in front of ten or so guys washing and talking. I am there, really there and yet not completely, in this moment that has the hazy contours of a dream. I recognize Yann Moreau in the back, on the left, his back turned to me. Soap suds cover his head, cascade over his shoulder blades, form a line that runs down his back and slides between his butt cheeks until it melds into the soapy puddle that covers the floor. My breathing accelerates; my mouth goes dry.

I should clear out. Has anyone seen me? Get out of here, Colin, you damn fool. I can already hear them shouting at me. Get the hell out, Colin.

: :

At home, I masturbate twice, eyes closed on that moment from which I want to extract every last detail. On that moment that is quickly fading away, that is already evaporating.

36
THEATRE CITY

BETWEEN SCHOOL, the knick-knack shop and my evenings spent fantasizing about Yann Moreau and making him laugh on MSN—he finds everything I say funny as hell, so I lay it on thick, hoping to make myself indispensable—time is flying by at the speed of sound.

December 19 arrives, the last day of class before the holidays. It's also English immersion day, and each team is set to present its city project. Catherine Crosnier and I have been preparing for ages: our poster is perfect, and we've been rehearsing our oral presentation at lunch every day for a week.

As fate would have it, Eugénie and Catherine Julien are the ones to break the ice. Their city is called Rainbowia (which everyone, including them, finds impossible to pronounce) and owes its name to the fact that it's entirely multicoloured. It makes for a flashy poster, but honestly, I find the concept weak. A rainbow city, so what? What's the point? It's not great. It must have been Catherine

Julien's idea. Regardless, they do well on the oral presentation. Eugénie's good mood seems to have relaxed Catherine Julien, who ventures a few jokes in English, despite usually keeping a low profile. But when a reject makes a joke, no one laughs; it's a sad rule that every good high school student must respect.

On her way back to her desk, Eugénie passes close to me.

"Good job!" I whisper.

She doesn't even look at me. Is she friends with Catherine Julien now? Has she abandoned me, replaced me? That'll teach me. Without Eugénie, I'm not much.

Now it's Guillaume Piché and Guillaume Langlois' turn to present their city: Sexytown. At first, they'd named it Sextown, but Ms. Parker had vetoed that. On their big, ugly poster, you can see where they had to add the Y in a hurry. They should have taken the time to start over. It's a big mess, but what else can you expect from those two idiots?

Their oral presentation is both bad (they haven't memorized their text) and good (they're popular guys, so everything they say triggers amused reactions from the class—another sad rule).

They're followed by Catherine Wagner and Guillaume Dionne (Olympic City, good work, boring presentation) and then Catherine Pronovost and Catherine Laramée (Horseville, original idea, disjointed presentation and half-coloured poster).

Finally, just before the break, it's our turn to present Theatre City. With clammy hands, I place our poster on the blackboard ledge. Catherine Crosnier is wearing her habitual gloomy expression. But as soon as she begins speaking, she lights up.

"Hello, citizens of Quebec! We come from a town far, far away, where entertainment is king. We come from . . ."

In unison and gesticulating like actors: "Theatre City!"

Ms. Parker seems impressed. That encourages me.

"Theatre City is a large city with more than two million inhabitants. It is located in a beautiful valley near the Pacific Ocean," I continue.

"And can you guess why it's called Theatre City?" Catherine Crosnier asks.

She pretends to survey the class. "Yes, you guessed right! Because it's the entertainment capital of the Earth!"

Her voice drips with fake enthusiasm; it doesn't suit her. But oral presentations are the height of fake, that's just how it is.

My turn to act. "With more than fifty playhouses, twenty movie theatres and ten concert halls, Theatre City attracts tourists from all over the world in search of the best time of their lives."

And so on, and blah blah blah for seven minutes, until the grand finale, when Catherine Crosnier and I take out two top hats from a bag, put them on and awkwardly tap dance to "Singin' in the Rain"—my teammate's idea "to make us stand out." I notice Eugénie laughing hysterically in the back; Guillaume Langlois seems totally disgusted, and even Catherine Julien is looking down at her desk. The other students clap half-heartedly. Damn.

As we return to our seats, I catch a murmur but can't tell where it's coming from. "That was *so gay*."

I feel myself burning from head to toe. I spend the rest of the day trying to disappear; Eugénie spends it avoiding me. Things are going very well.

::

Yo! :) My stepsister told me your
oral went well. Cool!

Catherine Crosnier certainly didn't tell him about the fiasco of the tap number. I quiver with shame just thinking about it. I act casual:

Me: *LOL! It was OK. Both of us are*
pretty good in English.
Him: *I'm sure you were great!: P*

I savour his little compliment before replying:

Me: *And you? How was your day?*
Him: *Good, I'm on vacation, too!*
For almost a month . . .
Me: *What are you going to do for all that time?*
LOL

A minute passes before he writes:

See you, I hope! ;)

Shit. If this guy isn't in love with me, he's sure acting like it.

37

BULGARIAN FILMS SUBTITLED IN SPANISH

YANN MOREAU KEEPS HIS PROMISE; the next day he invites me to the movies.

I want to see the latest instalment of *Lord of the Rings* at StarCité, but Yann asks me to meet him at Le Clap. They're showing a movie I've never heard of but that he's dying to show me: *Lost in Translation*. He doesn't have to ask twice. For him, I would watch Bulgarian films subtitled in Spanish every night for the rest of my life.

The bus lets me off in front of the Pyramide shopping centre. I'm beginning to regret not getting my driver's licence over the summer. Then I could suggest impromptu outings, too, and start being more independent. Now I'm stuck getting jostled on the always-packed number 7 that stops every fifteen metres. Public transportation is for children and poor people, especially in the winter. Yann Moreau gets around in a Volvo or a BMW.

In the lobby of Le Clap, he's practically vibrating. He loves movies, and his passion is a pleasure to behold. At the same time, it breaks my heart, because soon he'll have to exile himself to Montreal to pursue it.

"This is my second time seeing it. It's such a captivating film, Colin! You're going to love it. Besides, the music is wild."

His movie pick doesn't appeal to me much, but seeing Yann Moreau in such a good mood is enough to make me happy.

In front of the concession stand, I ask, "Want some popcorn?"

He looks me up and down strangely. "I prefer to concentrate on the film when I go to the movies."

Damn, I've committed another gaffe. "Oh, I understand. Me, too, actually."

He replies immediately, like he realizes he's been a jerk. "Have some! It's fine. It's just . . . I don't want any, but you should have some."

I call him a snob. We laugh.

The theatre is small, and there are only four old ladies seated in the middle. We choose spots in the last row. When we're seated, he turns to me. "So what's your favourite movie?"

I pretend to think about it, but I already know the answer. "*Titanic*."

His eyes widen. "For real?"

I was going to admit that I have the box set at home, that I've watched the first video at least fifty times and the second one maybe twenty times, but instead I counter, "What? Do you think it's bad?"

"No, there's no wrong answer! What do you like about the movie?"

The sublime Jack Dawson. Kate Winslet's doe eyes. The scene where he draws her on the couch. Céline's song.

"The period costumes," I say simply.

Suddenly, he's taking me seriously. "Oh yes, those were very well done."

Another idea comes into my head. "And the love story," I venture.

Yann Moreau smiles, knocks his shoulder against mine. "So you're a romantic?"

I go bright red, which I hope doesn't show in the relative darkness of the cinema. I lob the question back to him. "I don't know . . . are you?"

He looks down, runs his hand through his hair, doesn't say anything else. The awkwardness is delicious, but I'm incapable of maintaining it.

"So, what about you? What's your favourite movie?"

"It's impossible to choose . . ."

It's my turn to shake him up a bit. "Try! I told you mine."

He falls silent and takes three centuries to think about it. The theatre lights are starting to dim when he finally answers me. "Anyway, these days it's *Les Glaneurs et la Glaneuse.*"

The what and the what? Honestly, I think he just invented a movie title. I modestly admit that I've never heard of it.

"It's a really cool documentary by Agnès Varda," he whispers. "We'll watch it together. Enjoy the movie!"

A documentary? Who watches documentaries?

::

I spent the entire movie focused on my right calf, which was touching his left leg. He couldn't have *not* felt it; he must have known our bodies were touching. And his leg didn't move one centimetre the whole time.

The film seemed fine to me, hypnotic, even though I couldn't see what Scarlett Johansson's character found in Bill Murray's.

As soon as the lights went on, Yann Moreau turned to me. "Tell me that doesn't make you want to go to Tokyo!"

I nodded vigorously while the electric guitar from "J'irai où tu iras" resonated in my head.

::

In his mother's gleaming BMW, we wait for the engine to warm up. I ask Yann if he likes driving.

"Nah!"

What does he mean, "nah"? Driving is freedom, comfort, independence and the future. But he thinks the opposite.

"Cars just mean more air pollution. They take up space on the streets for nothing. They're the past. They're an aberration." He keeps going. "Besides, in a place like Quebec City that has a public transportation system, having a car is pointless."

It's obvious this guy has never waited an hour for the 13. His argument perplexes me.

"Why do you always borrow your mother's car, then?"

He wriggles in his seat. "Yeah, I know. I'm a walking contradiction. Don't you have any contradictions?"

"No."

He laughs.

"What's your real father's name?" I ask.

"Jacques Moreau. He works in Ottawa. I don't see him much."

"Ottawa is the capital of Canada."

He doesn't answer, just looks at me with his twinkling eyes. It feels like we're about to kiss. Does he want the same thing as me? No one moves. Maybe a debate about cars followed by a question about his father isn't the ideal prelude to a kiss.

After a moment, I speak. "You know, earlier, I told you that my favourite movie was *Titanic*, but . . ."

Yann Moreau fidgets. “Sorry if I had a crappy reaction. You have the right to like *Titanic*. It’s a good blockbuster.”

“I know. But I think my second-favourite movie is *Moulin Rouge*.”

He makes an adorable face. “I haven’t seen it yet!”

“It’s messed up, but Ewan McGregor and Nicole Kidman are unbelievable.”

Yann Moreau adds, “Not to mention the love story . . .”

He’s turned to face me.

“Not to mention the love story,” I repeat.

We smile at one another.

38

INCEST

EUGÉNIE BUJOLD IS STILL MY BEST FRIEND. My one-and-only, great, excellent friend. Since I don't want to end up alone in the world, and since Yann Moreau might not ever love me as much as I love him, I have to think of Eugénie. Love cannot overshadow friendship. Especially a friendship that's as strong and as old as ours.

So, on this December 22, before the Christmas festivities begin and we're monopolized by family dinners, I invite her for a walk in Old Quebec.

She meets me at my place, and from there we go out to wait for the number 7. The bus ride passes in uncomfortable silence: I'm trying to figure out how to approach Eugénie, how to start a conversation that is neither too serious nor too flippant.

We walk from Place D'Youville to City Hall in the same silence. On rue De Buade, the heady music from the Christmas shop masks our awkwardness for a while.

At the passage du Chien-d'Or, a little girl trips on the steps and hurts herself badly. Her parents, panicking, whisk her away; that's when the silence is finally broken. Of course, Eugénie speaks first, and what she says gives me goosebumps.

"I think I understand what's going on with you."

Impossible.

"Are you in love, Colin Bourque?"

Well. Who knew? She's actually guessed it. It's the dream scenario. I won't have to say it; my best friend—truer, braver and more upstanding than I—will do it for me. In a few seconds, everything will change: I won't be alone anymore.

Looking down, I nod.

"Are you in love with Catherine Crosnier?"

Shit. She's totally missed the mark. Why is she assuming I'm in love with that girl? I'm completely stuck. Do I lie? Again? Run away? I want to jump in the river. Seeing my hesitation, Eugénie continues.

"I knew it. I started to suspect you had a thing for her when you teamed up for the English project."

God, I feel the vomit rising in my throat—not at the thought of dating Catherine Crosnier, but because Eugénie's theory is pushing my back up against the wall. Sooner or later, she is going to force me to contradict her, to clear everything up, to explain the situation in detail. I'm regretting the mystery and the silence, which suddenly seem very desirable to me.

But my friend isn't finished.

"Then, when you stopped talking to me on MSN, it all made sense. When you're in love, you just want to be with the other person. It's natural." Her voice is choked with emotion. "Except I ended up alone, like a fool. I thought you had ditched me. I pictured myself finishing high school without you, having to find other friends."

On the word "friends," she bursts into tears. And I cry, too; I cry with her. Nearby, a few uncomfortable tourists move away.

: :

Sitting at a table in a crêpe spot on rue Saint-Jean, Eugénie and I drink hot chocolate in silence. I haven't admitted anything to her yet, but I understand, now, that the moment has come. Eugénie deserves my respect, and I need her in my life. I have no choice. Very slowly, I begin the discussion.

"You were right, Eug, when you said I'm in love."

She puts down her cup and looks at me intently. She is waiting. This is it, the moment has arrived. I can't turn back now; I have to break my years of silence and reach out to my best friend. My eyes fill with tears.

"But I'm not in love with Catherine Crosnier."

Eugénie's gaze is gentle.

"I'm in love with someone else." It feels like I'll never be able to say it. In a broken voice, I explain. "This is hard for me."

She takes my hand; a tear slides down her cheek. "Take your time, my friend."

The couple sitting at the next table is completely silent; I'm sure they're listening, and I'm mortified. But my decision is made: I will not leave here without telling Eugénie everything.

So I inhale deeply and blurt out, "It's Yann Moreau."

Her eyes widen. "Who?"

"Yann Moreau."

Eugénie smiles kindly. "Okay. So it's a boy?"

Hiccupping with emotion, I nod my head. Unbelievable. It's done. It's said; it's over. I am no longer all alone on this earth. Wiping away the tears that have returned to blur my vision, I explain, "He's Catherine Crosnier's stepbrother, the one who's on the swim team with Clément."

"Oh!" She seems glad. "That's good news! My best friend is in love with a swimmer! And what about him, does he love you back?"

I shrug. After all, I don't really care. At this moment, the relief and pride of having spoken up are overshadowing everything else.

"But isn't he your brother's girlfriend's brother?" Eugénie exclaims.

I nod.

"Er . . . that's incest, Colin."

"Dumbass!"

We laugh like idiots, holding each other's hands. I should have fallen in love with her instead.

39

NOBODY'S BIRTHDAY

CHRISTMAS IS MY DAY.

In fact, it's everyone's day, because we don't celebrate anyone in particular. Anyway, that's the case in my family. There's a nativity scene under the tree, but we don't spare the slightest thought for baby Jesus. And no one needs to sit in front of a cake while the others sing and stare at them. Christmas doesn't make any sense, has no logic and no real reason for being. It's nobody's birthday. It's perfect.

Mainly, it's a day of make-believe. The houses and the city are decorated like movie sets; people wear clothes they consider elegant (the ladies take out their sequins and the gentlemen dress like lawyers). Music plays on every corner; delicious dishes are lined up on kitchen counters; snowflakes fall from the sky . . .

In short, it's a day when everything is fake. And if there is one thing that I've understood, this year, it's that I'm as fake as everyone else. So Christmas is my day.

::

Clément is fooling around in his room with Catherine Moreau. From time to time, they burst out laughing like they're tickling one another. It nauseates me a bit. My mother is preparing the meal. I'm watching the snow fall from the living room window. The street lights turn on quietly. Céline sings "Another Year Has Gone By" and "Happy Xmas (War is Over)." Magic takes hold.

My father's Toyota pulls into the driveway. He went to pick up Matante Pauline, who has been spending Christmas Eve with us for the past two years, since all my grandparents died. They were all in a plane crash together . . . No, I'm joking; they all died in different ways, several years apart.

Spending the evening of December 24 with us delights Matante Pauline, who would otherwise be bruising her tailbone on a church pew. And for us, it means having an old person in the house. Christmas is a holiday for old people: without them, a little something would be missing.

My great-aunt walks into the house, puts down her coat and kisses me on both cheeks. "Merry Christmas, dear Colin. What a nice outfit you have on! Have you ever seen anything like it? The people are so well-dressed on avenue de Cherbourg . . ."

She gives me a mischievous wink. You'd think she's been drinking, but I'm pretty sure she's just excited to see us. Her dress isn't bad either: a kind of curtain fabric in burgundy tones, adorned with a gold peacock brooch. Matante Pauline smells of old lady's perfume. The scent of flower beds. I love it.

She rushes to help my mother in the kitchen. My father, on top of the world, walks around the house taking drink orders. I hear my brother's girlfriend ask for champagne—does she think we're millionaires?—before settling for a glass of white wine. My brother wants a beer, and the three adults are drinking half-and-halfs. I ask for a glass of Tropical Passion juice with ice.

Marie-Louise enters the living room with a plate of smoked salmon appetizers. She's wearing a new black dress she bought at The Bay—simple and elegant. Soon, everyone joins us for cocktail hour.

: :

At around seven o'clock, we sit down at the table. My mother has prepared a beautiful feast: meat pies, sausages in maple syrup, stuffed rolls, salads, cheeses, bread and grapes.

I'm starting to get fed up with my brother and his girlfriend's whispers and caresses. They never take their hands off each other; it's like they think they're alone at the table. Are they drunk? Their behaviour is almost sexual, but my parents say nothing. At Christmas, no one wants to argue.

Fortunately, Matante Pauline is there to distract us with her stories of the olden days.

"When I was a girl in Saint-Basile . . ."

"In my day, at school . . ."

"Years ago on rang Sainte-Angélique . . ."

"Back then, at midnight mass . . ."

I listen attentively, nodding often. Old people were born before the invention of the Discman, and they have the memory of an elephant. I can't even remember what happened last year.

When my mother brings in dessert (a chocolate yule log and fruit salad), Matante Pauline, perhaps prompted by my brother and his girlfriend's fondling, focuses her attention on me.

"What about you, Colin? Do you have a girlfriend at school?"

This question is tantamount to torture for me. I always reply honestly but feel like I'm lying by omission, and I hate that. I'm afraid of blushing, stammering, saying too much. I feel cowardly and terribly fake.

I turn to Matante Pauline and answer as naturally as possible. "No."

Clément murmurs something in Catherine Moreau's ear. She practically lies down on him and giggles hysterically. That's it, I'm fed up. I can't hold back anymore.

"Can't you guys let go of each other for two seconds?"

"Colin!" my father scolds.

"What? Are you jealous?" my brother bites back.

Catherine Moreau, half drunk, chooses this instant to plant a big, wet kiss on Clément's mouth. It's too much for me.

"Jealous of what, you fucking idiot?" I burst out.

Matante Pauline starts and clutches her chest.

"Come on, Colin! It's Christmas!" my mother cries.

My brother takes advantage of the awkwardness I've created to cross the line. "Come on, Colin, it's Christmas! If you want to make out with someone, just find some guy at your school!"

"Colin! Uh, not Colin. I mean, Clément!" my father stammers.

Whenever he mixes up his sons like that, it means he's experiencing inner turmoil. Something flashes before my eyes. I see red. It isn't possible. What has just been said can't have been said. I look down and feel everyone else doing the same.

Seething with shame, I leave the table to go hide in my room.

::

I hear my parents telling off Clément. As an old lady, Matante Pauline must be shocked. What a shitty evening.

Marie-Louise knocks on my door. "Colin? Your brother has something to tell you, sweetheart."

Clément's voice reaches me through the door, terse. "I'm sorry."

What is he sorry for? For having ruined Christmas? I'm the one who ruined it. My brother simply said what he was thinking, deep down. His apologies are only making things worse, because they confirm that he was thinking something unbearable, that *my reality* is unbearable.

I don't answer Clément. My mother asks me to return to the table; I say that they can continue without me. I can't imagine leaving my room and facing everyone's embarrassment. The conversation that could settle everything cannot take place. No one wants to hear it tonight.

::

After an hour of brooding, I gather all my courage and hurriedly leave my room. I walk past the living room; my father says something to me and points to an armchair, but I ignore him and take refuge in the basement, in front of the computer. Yann Moreau is signed in to MSN. My heart pounding, I write:

Are you there?

A minute goes by before he answers:

Yeah. I'm bored.

I sigh with relief.

Me: *That sucks! :(*
Him: *Nah, it's not serious. I'm reading in my room. We're having our family Christmas dinner tomorrow, seeing as my sister is at your place!*
Me: *LOL*

I am seeking comfort but don't know how to express it. He writes back:

You? You having a nice evening?

My eyes mist over.

Me: *Not really . . .*
Him: *Oh! Sorry . . . Is there anything I can do? :(*
Me: *I want to talk to you.*
Can we meet somewhere?
Him: *Yeah, no problem*
Me: *At Sainte-Geneviève Park?*
Him: *I'm on my way!*

I have butterflies in my stomach. Despite my sadness, shame and anger, I feel like part of me is pleased by the turn of events. Being sad, with a little luck, also means being consoled. I blow my nose loudly, go upstairs to slip on my coat and, under my family's devastated gaze, announce that I'm going out for a walk.

"Come on, Clément... Uh, not Clément, Colin!" my father calls out.

Again! My father must be deeply troubled. But I can't help him: I'm the one who needs help. I leave the house and, with a light, melancholy snow falling, head to the park.

40

SAINTE-GENEVIÈVE PARK

ALONE NEAR THE SOFTBALL FIELD, I admire the lights of the northern section of the city, below Sainte-Geneviève Park. One day, one of those lights will be mine. It will illuminate the life that I'll have built, an authentic life.

The crunching of snow informs me of Yann Moreau's arrival. Hands in his coat pockets, he smiles at me.

"Hey!" I say.

"Hey!" he replies.

I don't know how to begin talking about what just happened at home without revealing my feelings for him. It's an awkward situation. He doesn't seem to know what to say either, so we size each other up out of the corners of our eyes while kicking a snowbank.

Finally, I turn to him. He looks up. "What's going on?"

"I don't know."

He gives a small, forced laugh. "What do you mean, you don't know?"

"I don't know what's been going on since . . ."

Silence.

"Since what?" he asks.

My throat is dry. In one breath I answer, "Since I met you."

Yann stands completely still. "What do you mean?"

I sigh. "You don't know what I mean?"

His beautiful eyes are focused on me. Beneath the white glow of the floodlights, I feel exposed, like an insect on a microscope slide. But no one is watching us; Yann Moreau and I are alone in the park, on Christmas Eve.

"Yes, I think I know what you mean," he says.

My breathing quickens. Can it be? Tonight, I need to be sure. "No, I don't think that you . . ." I trail off.

"Yes, Colin, I swear. I know what you mean." He approaches. He's going to hit me. I deserve it; I need it. I stiffen. Our bodies are almost touching.

"Have you ever kissed anyone?" Yann Moreau asks. I shake my head, short of breath. "Would you like it if we kissed?"

My heart stops beating. Something unthinkable and impossible is happening to me.

Slowly, I nod. Yann takes my hand, moves his face closer to mine. The precise moment his lips touch mine, I lose contact with reality.

We kiss for a long time, without stopping, almost without breathing, and the only times I remove my face from his are to check that my feet are still on the ground, that I haven't left my earthly body to enter heaven.

When finally, after a millennium, we release one another, Yann Moreau smiles at me. "I've been wanting to do that for a month."

"Two months for me," I reply.

We laugh. And we kiss again, again, again . . . I am dying to say all sorts of things, but the many love stories in my TV shows have taught me the importance of showing independence and indifference to make yourself desirable, so I say nothing. But as we're about to head back toward his car, it's Yann Moreau who takes my head between his hands.

"I love you," he murmurs.

41

MY UNRESOLVED SITUATION

WHEN I GET HOME, I am surprised to find my brother and my parents sitting in the living room. The clock says twelve thirty; I've been gone for more than two hours.

With Yann, I was invincible. Here, my situation is unresolved. I have only one wish: to climb into bed and replay in my head every second, every sound, every smell and every sensation from my meeting with Yann.

But my mother says, "Colin, are you okay?"

I don't want to talk. I nod in silence. My father frowns.

"Would you like to sit down with us?"

I shake my head. My brother looks sorry. Marie-Louise is rubbing her hands like she just put on hand cream. She is nervous. "My prince, if you have something to tell us . . ."

No! *You* talk to *me*, set me free! Tell me who I am, what I am. Don't you see that I can't? Don't you sense the impenetrability of my gaze, all those shadows moving around behind the curtain?

Silence remains my most reliable shield, my most convincing lie. Sometimes, you have to know how to lie. Everyone lies to their parents.

My father sighs. “Okay . . . We’ll unwrap the gifts tomorrow.”

As I turn around to go to my room, my mother adds, “We love you.”

I nod in reply. I know they love me. They know how much I love them. But I am trying to love myself as well.

42

NICOLE KIDMAN, HALF-DEAD

ON THE MORNING of December 25, on avenue de Cherbourg, everyone has returned to their role, myself included. We unwrapped the gifts before breakfast, like when I was little.

I got three books (including the most recent *Harry Potter*), a computer game (*Diablo II*), and a man's watch. I had asked for money, but my parents think that's too lame a gift. Eugénie stopped by to give me hers: a Desjardins T-shirt that her father got from work. Yann Moreau would find that a weird gift. Desjardins is surely part of the capitalist system. I like it. I am encouraging a Quebec company.

The family festivities will start up again on December 31. Until then, I have lots of time to read, play on the computer and think about Yann Moreau.

::

On December 27, Eugénie calls to invite Yann and me for a movie night in her basement. I immediately make a beeline for my *Moulin Rouge* DVD, thrilled to be able to introduce Yann Moreau to this extraordinary movie. I know Eugénie loves it, too.

I scarf down my dinner before heading to my friend's place. Walking over, I run my hand over the snowbanks cut at right angles by the snowplow. White walls line the street.

At the corner of Lavallée and de Strasbourg, Yann is waiting for me, kicking a block of ice. I join him. He smiles at me behind his neck warmer and takes my hand briefly.

"You didn't borrow your mother's car?"

"No, I took the bus. I'm trying to be consistent."

I certainly didn't ask that of him, given how inconsistent I am!

At Eugénie's, Yann Moreau introduces himself to my best friend—she's smiling from ear to ear—and to her parents, for whom he's just a new friend. He makes a good impression. Everyone likes this boy. I think of the day when my family might meet him. It is a faraway, blurry scene, like in a science fiction movie.

The three of us get comfortable in front of the television with chips, Glosettes and Sunny Delight.

I spend the first half-hour of the movie watching Yann, seeking the sparkle in his eyes, a hint that will reveal what he thinks of *Moulin Rouge*; that will confirm that he and I are made to get along. But what if he hates it? I would not survive. I'm sweating; my feet are cold. Film, music, art—they carry a lot of weight.

During "Elephant Love Medley," my eyes fill with tears. It's too beautiful, too romantic. I watch Yann Moreau; he doesn't move a muscle.

In the middle of the movie, Eugénie gets up to go to the bathroom. Yann grabs me by the shoulders, draws me in to him and plants a million kisses on my neck.

"I've been wanting to do that so badly. I've been thinking of you this whole time."

I'm in paradise. Life is worth living when Yann Moreau is breathing on your neck. I turn toward him and we kiss for as long as we can, until Eugénie comes back down.

At the end of the movie, when Nicole Kidman, half-dead and weeping, breaks into "Come What May" on the stage of the Moulin Rouge to win back Ewan McGregor, I glance at Yann. A fat tear is running down his cheek. Relief.

After the movie is over, he declares it to be a super beautiful postmodern film. I don't know what he means, and I don't care. I've found my soul mate.

::

It's after ten o'clock. Yann and I are walking up the street toward chemin Sainte-Foy. Every deserted street corner plays host to us for several minutes. We cling to one another with our mittens and make out till we're breathless.

The walk to the bus stop, which is less than a kilometre, takes us over an hour. On the number 7, Yann sits down next to a window and draws a heart in the frost. Only for me.

I walk home slowly, drunk on my no longer completely secret love.

43
IMMORTALITY

THE KNICK-KNACK SHOP no longer exists. A few days ago, Claudette Hallé phoned me to explain that she'd decided to close the Sainte-Foy branch. The old ladies in the neighbourhood will have to procure their trinkets elsewhere. I only worked there for six months, which still felt like a lifetime to me. I would have really liked for Claudette to offer me the Heart of the Ocean as a souvenir. She'll probably keep it for herself, wear it and admire herself in the bathroom mirror. Lucky.

The knick-knack shop hasn't survived Manon Sirois, great lover of puppets, Pierrots and baubles of all sorts. Deep down, Manon was a good boss. A decent boss. I will never forget her. In any case, not for quite a while. My homage is pitiful, but as usual, ideas and words escape me. I have no talent for serious things. It's the intention that counts.

Nevertheless, my sorrow has shifted. Before, I would cry, imagining Manon Sirois dying in a hospital room and her elderly mother devastated by the loss of her child. Now, I know that even the worst things have an ending. For Manon, the worst is over. And I no longer want to feel bad about something that has already happened, that is already over.

December 31, 2003. In my earphones, the most beautiful song of all is playing: Céline Dion's duet with the Bee Gees, "Immortality." Eugénie says Céline is imitating the Bee Gees' style. True, she makes her voice sound really breathy—to adapt, be part of the group. I get it. But her true essence shines through when she sings her long note. And the sincerity with which she delivers the last sentence of the song gives me the chills:

With all my love for you
And what else we may do
We don't say goodbye

44

FUCK

VACATION IS ALMOST OVER. Soon I'll have to go back to school, that place where everything is normal, where everything is fine, that machine in which I am a satisfied cog, that place that is like me, where what I am and what I present to the world are one and the same. I excel at the art of pretending that high school hasn't almost broken me in two.

Today, Yann is staying home alone while his family has gone skiing in Stoneham. And he's invited me to spend the day with him. On my way out, I thought of lying, saying I was going to Eugénie's, but simply told my father, "I'm going somewhere. I'll be home later."

He looked taken aback. I slammed the door.

::

Stretched out facing one another on his mattress, we speak softly.

"It's good that you told Eugénie. I haven't told anyone," Yann says.

I place my hand on his cheek.

"My best friends are on the swim team and I'm afraid they'll get on my case."

Our legs are intertwined on his bed.

"And my family . . ." he continues. Big sigh. "When I was little, I saw this show with my parents where two men kissed. And my father said 'ugh.' Just ugh, like that: ugh! We kept watching like nothing happened. They've long forgotten about it. Not me. I know my parents would accept me for who I am; I know they love me. I know them well enough to know that. But I can still hear my father saying 'ugh.' It's fucked up, eh? Just a little 'ugh.'"

"It's your father who was fucked up."

A tear escapes from the corner of his eye onto the duvet. I hug him against me. His distress affects me even more because I share it. Talking to Eugénie lifted a weight from my shoulders, but I soon realized I'd always have to do it over again. There will always be someone I'll have to tell, someone I'll have to open myself up to.

Yann Moreau says, "Anyway, I'm sure my parents know. Or they suspect. They think I've changed. I even talked to them about giving up swimming."

I'm not so sure. "They must think you're taking drugs. The minute they notice something different, parents immediately picture their kid taking drugs."

He sighs. “Next year, if I move to Montreal, it’ll be easier.”

This idea shakes me up, but I understand what he means. To remind myself there are good reasons for living, I bury my face in Yann’s brown hair—it enchants me. The sun falling over us makes me drowsy. We end up falling asleep in each other’s arms.

: :

When I wake up, I can no longer feel my legs. I gently push Yann, sit up and place my feet on the ground. The clock indicates noon. We still have lots of time before his family returns.

Yann yawns. Curled up in a ball on his yellow duvet, he reminds me of a little lion that I love, that I adore. I want him to know everything about me. I dream that people know everything about me. Almost everything. Loving Yann Moreau means starting anew.

“I have something to confess.”

He rubs his eyes, sits up.

“I’m a fan.”

“A fan?”

“A fan.”

“A fan of what?”

I take a deep breath. “Céline Marie Claudette Dion.”

“What? Who?”

"Seriously, are you listening to me? Don't make me say it again."

"Do you mean Céline Dion?"

"That's right."

He laughs. Mortification. "What did you call her?"

"Céline Marie Claudette Dion."

A new peal of laughter. "You're crazy, Colin. Why do you call her that?"

I don't know. Because it's her real name. Because it's her real name and at the same time, it isn't. Because I can't help but lie, even in my confessions. The "Marie Claudette" between the "Céline" and the "Dion" confuses people, masks the embarrassment. Is he making fun of me? I feel like I have no answer to anything. Everything is difficult to say; everything feels like an admission.

"So you won't laugh at me," I reply.

"You really take me for a snob."

I have my reasons! "Everything you like is cool. Your favourite movie is *Les Glandeurs et la Glandeuse.*"

"Glaneurs! Glaneuse! Idiot!" he cries.

We laugh. His arms encircle me, and I continue. "Céline is the opposite of cool. But that's how it is—I didn't set out to love her. I didn't set out to be ashamed of it either. I have no control over anything, fuck!"

Since I've been in love, I've been swearing like a sailor. Yann puts his chin on my shoulder. "We are who we are, fuck!" And he kisses my neck. "I don't really know Céline Dion's music. But I'm excited for you to share it with me."

::

Yann Moreau goes upstairs to the living room to get the only Céline CD his family owns—*D'eux*, of course. He inserts it in the stereo before joining me on the bed.

"Is this okay, as a soundtrack?" he asks, a bit jokingly, but not entirely.

And all of a sudden, it hits me: I'm going to sleep with a boy. With Yann Moreau. With Jack from *Titanic*. I go into a trance, a bit like that time in the pool locker room; I picture Yann again in the shower, his back studded with moles, the soapy water running between his butt cheeks. I also picture Eugénie's father in his briefs, with his beard and his hairy chest. Around us, the room blurs.

::

We kissed to "Pour que tu m'aimes encore." During "Regarde-moi," we undressed. To "Cherche encore," we came while telling each other *I love you.*

::

I examine the shapes that Yann Moreau's semen makes on my belly.

"What's going to happen now?" I wonder aloud.

He takes my face between his hands. "We date each other. If you want."

"But in secret?"

He lets "J'attendais" go by and declares, "I really like that song. I like its gentleness."

I smile.

"In secret?" he continues. "Yeah, maybe. Why not? It's not our fault if there's stuff that isn't obvious, if the two of us aren't obvious. I'd like it if everyone already knew. One day, something will happen, they'll find out . . . I only want to think about you, about us. Not about them. It's not a big deal, what we're doing. Or what we are. It's other people who make it into a much bigger deal."

Pensive, I nod. To keep silent—to lie, really—is painful. But speaking out requires courage. Gathering your courage takes time. And my patience has its limits. Love is here, now, in my arms, asking to be made.

Yann concludes, "Colin, we have the right to keep our mouths shut. People can go to hell. We love each other. Barf! I sound like a song . . ."

"By Céline Dion? Almost."

No. Céline never tells people to go to hell in her songs, even if sometimes she should.

He laughs. I place my lips on his chest.

"What do you say, handsome? Fuck the world?" he asks.

The clouds part; the sky above widens; a ray of sunlight blinds me, and I just manage to whisper, before feeling his hand on my penis, before he glues his mouth to mine and our tongues mingle, "Fuck the damn world."

45
BURKINA FASO

IT'S ALL WELL AND GOOD to tell the whole planet to go to hell, but that doesn't stop classes from starting up again. Even though this Monday marks the end of the most beautiful time of the year, I go back to school with my heart lighter than usual. I, Colin Bourque, have made love. Against all expectations. Despite the fact my body doesn't look like much at all, despite the pimples on my cheeks and my stupid expression, I slept with a boy. And not just any boy. An eighteen-year-old swimmer who says *I love you.*

Movies, television and adults in general teach teenagers, especially girls, that the circumstances of their first sexual encounter will determine their worth as a person. You have to make love at just the right moment (not too soon because that's traumatic, and not too late because that's humiliating, with sixteen being considered the ideal age), with the right person (attractive, desirable and loveable), all while respecting yourself (waiting to be "ready"). During my entire teens, I pictured having my first sexual encounter in my late twenties, with a sleazy man who would lick my body while I shivered with revulsion.

But no. For once, I fit in perfectly. Or almost.

::

Today at noon, I was waiting in line for the microwave, in the school cafeteria, when Catherine Pronovost declared, "My cousin's name is Rebecca and she lives on Rebecca Street. Imagine!"

To which Catherine Bernier replied, "Well, my name is Catherine Bernier, and I used to live in Bernières. That's not much better!"

I could have tried to go one better, but I don't live on rue de la Colline or in Burkina Faso. The two other students in the microwave line, little kids in Grade 7, stared at them, wide-eyed. When you're in Grade 7 you observe the big kids in Grade 11, telling yourself that later on, you'll be like them. I know, I was the same.

Since I've slept with Yann Moreau, I feel taller, more mature and independent. To the rest of the world, it's imperceptible, but the discussion between Catherine Pronovost and Catherine Bernier in the microwave line confirms it: I don't think I'll talk like that anymore. I think I've changed. A Rebecca who lives on Rebecca Street no longer seems so extraordinary to me. I've moved on. I'm evolving. And if I go by Hollywood conventions, I'm evolving for the better.

Good lord, I even impress myself.

46

PROJECTING

ON WEDNESDAY EVENING, Marie-Louise, Daniel, Clément and I are sitting at the table eating peach meatballs. The telephone rings. My mother sighs.

"People who call during dinner . . ."

She gets up to answer. "Oh, hello, Ghislaine. Yes, I'm fine, yes . . . You? Oh, yeah? Oh? Oh! Congratulations . . ."

The discussion doesn't last more than two minutes. My mother repeats her congratulations three times, hangs up and returns to the table. My father, my brother and I stare at her as we chew our meatballs.

"That was Ghislaine Baril . . ."

We know!

"She called to say that her daughter had the baby last week. A boy."

I immediately look up at Clément. My brother is the same age as Ghislaine's daughter; the thought of having a baby at eighteen terrifies him, I'm sure. But his expression doesn't change. He scarcely reacts. Clément is so calm, so detached from everything. That's the privilege of normal guys. I envy him.

"What are they going to name him?" my father asks.

"Guillaume."

Of course.

Marie-Louise smiles and picks up her fork as if nothing happened.

I can't help myself. "She had him young, her Guillaume . . ."

"Honestly, Colin, what's it to you?" my mother asks, suddenly dismayed.

I scowl. "I was just saying that she had him young, that's all!"

My father jumps in. "You could be a bit less *judgmental* about other people, my boy. Don't you think?"

Incredible. When *I'm* the one who constantly feels judged!

Clément rubs it in. "Yeah, Colin, stop judging, you're no better than anyone else."

Before I have time to say something stupid back, Marie-Louise tries to close the debate.

"When a woman gives birth, you congratulate her, that's all. It's not up to us to judge her age or her situation; you congratulate her, then you hang up. The rest is not our business, not our problem. Is that clear?"

I roll my eyes. "Imagine if Clément had a baby with Catherine Moreau tomorrow morning. Would you call her to congratulate her?"

My mother drops her utensils on her plate and cries, "Clément's girlfriend doesn't work in a sandpaper factory!"

Jubilation. Jubilation! Marie-Louise has just been caught out being a snob. My brother, who really takes people at face value—I have to give him that—has failed to understand the implications of my mother's reply. "What does that have to do with it?" he frowns.

My mother clears her throat, adjusts her blouse and calmly replies,

"I mean that Catherine Moreau has professional ambitions incompatible with motherhood for the moment. Medical school is very demanding."

"Oh!"

Marie-Louise has gotten out of it too easily for me.

"That's not what you meant, admit it," I say. "You meant that Ghislaine Baril's daughter got pregnant at eighteen because that's how things work in her social class."

If there's one thing *Titanic* has taught me, it's that there are three social classes in the world. The third-class people drown at the bottom of the ship while the first-class ones make it off the boat. I don't exactly know what happens in second class.

Daniel, who I am beginning to exasperate, turns to me to defend his wife. "You're the one saying that, Colin. Stop projecting on your mother."

Huh? When my father starts to trot out his vocabulary, it's impossible to argue with him. His method of reminding me of my ignorance shuts me up for good.

"In any case, where are you going with this?" he barks.

Nowhere. I never go anywhere, anyway. But why are they questioning the existence of social classes? Those two would not have lasted long on board a luxury steamship in 1912.

47

A STAKE IN THE EYE

YANN MOREAU HAS GONE AWAY FOR THE WEEKEND; it's his stepsister's birthday, and they're all celebrating together at the Crosniers' in Rimouski.

So I've invited Eugénie to go sliding. I have a plastic saucer that flies over the snow at terrifying speeds, and she brought her three-ski sled, which is not as fast, but has the advantage of a steering wheel. Eugénie is terrified of sliding backwards and hitting a jump. The last thing she wants to do is break her neck.

At Sainte-Geneviève Park, just beside the softball field, there's a tall hill, tall enough that all the neighbourhood kids go there with their sleds. At sixteen, Eugénie and I are the oldest ones who still hang out there.

My best friend gets on her three-ski and gives herself a push; she hits a big sheet of ice that propels her forward at a phenomenal speed. She screams the whole way like someone has just driven a stake through her eye. The other children stop to watch her. I laugh my head off.

Eugénie takes forever to climb back up; she made it all the way to the fence at the edge of the park. I launch myself onto my saucer, which spins, spins, spins all the way to the bottom of the hill. I roll over on my back. The sky swims above me, completely white with clouds or snow.

A child shouts at me to get out of the way—he's going to run into me. I stand, start climbing back up. At the top of the hill, Eugénie is already ready to go again. I throw a snowball at her just as she flies past me, shouting, but I aim badly and hit a little kid in the back. I turn around, snorting.

::

After an hour, we've had enough of hanging around in the wet snow. I suggest that we go eat at Subtil, one of our favourite restaurants. Eugénie makes a face.

"I don't have any money. I can't go to restaurants whenever I want."

"My treat. I have lots of money left from the knick-knack shop. I have at least a thousand dollars in my account."

Eugénie whistles. "You're rich!"

At my house, she calls her parents to inform them of our plans while I hang our snowsuits up to dry. Clément and Catherine Moreau (who skipped the Rimouski trip) are watching TV in the living room; my brother's expression warns me that Eugénie and I are not welcome to join them. In any case, their show looks stupid.

::

The album *Unison* is playing on low in my room. My friend and I are absent-mindedly throwing a rubber ball that goes with a game that I lost all the pieces for a long time ago.

"Your money from the knick-knack store . . . Didn't you want to save it to go see Céline Dion in Las Vegas?" Eugénie asks.

I shrug. "Yeah . . . Maybe."

"A trip to Las Vegas must cost about a thousand bucks, right?"

"Yeah . . ."

I close my eyes for an instant, and Yann Moreau's face appears. It's like my ideas, my plans for 2003 belong to someone else. My life before resembles a black-and-white film. Now, as soon as silence falls, as soon as I settle in somewhere, I think about my boyfriend; I smell his shampoo. I wait only for his next kisses and plan nothing other than our next encounters.

"Colin? What are you thinking about?"

The rubber ball lands on my stomach. "About Yann."

My best friend tilts her head toward me and explains, like a teacher giving a lesson, "You know you can't forget about yourself? You know you're still a separate person?"

Great relationship advice from Miss Eugénie!

"What do you know about that?"

"I've seen that talk show hosted by the sex therapist."

"That's just a show for sex maniacs."

"No, it also talks about love and power dynamics!"

Power dynamics, now. How far are we going to take this nonsense?

Eugénie sits on my desk chair, clasps her hands and continues. "Yann Moreau is two years older than you; he's handsome, cultured and intelligent, so you admire him."

True.

"But your desires and dreams are just as worthwhile as his. You've been wanting to go to Las Vegas for a year. Don't give up on that! You love Céline so much . . ."

In the late nineties, Céline Dion did two world tours that stopped in Quebec City, but I was too young to even consider seeing her in concert. When you're a child, you aren't resourceful. Unfortunately, last year, Céline settled in the Nevada desert, which complicates things for her fans all over the world. At least her new show seems to be worth the detour.

I settle on the bed and declare, "It's not complicated: I'll find myself another job."

“To go see Céline in Las Vegas?”

Her insisting is really getting on my nerves. To pacify her, I give her an enormous smile. “Yes! Exactly!”

But I’m toying with another plan, a secret one: moving to Montreal for school, one day, to join Yann Moreau.

::

At Subtil, I watch the old couples eating at the nearby tables.

“What about you, have you ever been in love?”

Eugénie’s mouth is full of roast beef pita. A sip of peach juice helps her move it down her throat. “Well, in love . . . No, I don’t think so.”

My friend and I never talked about these things before I started going out with Yann, probably because I would have had to compromise myself to do so. But my love affair has opened up a whole new territory for our friendship.

What does Eugénie look like, objectively? Do boys find her beautiful? Personally, I like her so much that I can find no physical flaws. She’s just about perfect. But other guys have peculiar tastes. I’ve heard Guillaume Dionne say that Paris Hilton is the most beautiful woman in the world. Eugénie does not look one bit like Paris Hilton.

“I always thought you found Guillaume Brassard cute,” I casually suggest.

"No, you're projecting. You're the one who finds him cute."

That again! "Hey! My father said the same thing. Stop saying that I'm projecting. I don't even know what that means."

Her eyes widen. "You asked your father if he found Guillaume Brassard cute?"

"Do you think I'm an idiot? He said that about something else."

"Projecting is when you project something onto someone else. You're projecting your desire for Guillaume Brassard onto me."

I shrug. This is ridiculous. Where did Eugénie learn that? Certainly not from watching that sex therapy show. I should read more books. Céline Dion isn't going to teach me what projection is.

We finish our meal in silence. I suddenly have an idea and think I'm stupid not to have thought of it before. "Maybe you prefer girls."

My best friend smiles and places her hand on mine. "No, Colin. I'm normal."

"Fuck off."

She laughs. I laugh with her, even if the joke is cruel. Even if deep down I still have an impossible desire to be like all the other boys.

48

VERY FUCKED-UP MUSIC

LIFE AS A COUPLE IMPLIES being open to many things. To the ideas, habits and tastes of the loved one. If my boyfriend were a fan of Whitney Houston, Shania Twain or even Alanis Morissette, I would easily adapt to his music.

But Yann Moreau listens to Radiohead, Björk and Metric. I know Björk because I saw her in *Dancer in the Dark*, a messed-up movie that gave me nightmares for two days. But I never really paid attention to her music. Well, it's very fucked up.

This evening, Yann and I are meeting at the Monique-Corriveau Library. In a nook on the second floor, we sit down at a table piled high with books taken at random from the shelves. He brought his iPod. iPods are the future. Discmans are the past. Walkmans are prehistoric.

My boyfriend introduces me to all kinds of songs that he loves: "Creep," "Karma Police," "Go to Sleep," "Hyperballad," "Venus as a Boy," "Combat Baby," "Dead Disco." He also likes Dumas, which is fine: I already know *Le cours des jours*, an album my father listens to from time to time at home.

For now, I have to feign a degree of interest in his music. Maybe I'll get used to it someday.

After a particularly bizarre song by Björk, he looks at me, radiant, and whispers, "That shit is far-out. It's like music can't go any farther than that. It's the epitome of music."

I completely agree with him. For me, it is literally the epitome of a piece of shit. Is Yann Moreau pretending to like Céline Dion out of love for me? "The Power of Love" seems to me infinitely easier to appreciate than "All Is Full of Love."

: :

After the library closes, we dawdle on route de l'Église. I want to make love with Yann. That's all I want, every day. But it's complicated finding the right time and the right place. Clément and Catherine Moreau sleep together whenever they like, wherever they like, at our place, her place or anywhere else. With Yann and me, it's different.

We hide in a park and make out until we're trembling from the cold. So we separate and wait for the 800, on opposite sides of the street, waving to one another. His bus comes before mine. Through the window, he smiles at me. As the bus pulls away, I follow my Yann's black hat with my eyes.

49

RAGING TIGERS

CATHERINE JULIEN, the ultimate reject of Grade 11, is eating lunch alone at the end of a cafeteria table. She doesn't look sad or anxious or agitated. She is accustomed to her status. You can get used to anything. My mother taught me that, a few years ago, in reference to a bad haircut my brother had just gotten. Clément was crying, running his hands over his head. Marie-Louise took him in her arms and declared, "You'll get used to it. You can get used to anything."

My brother's hair quickly grew back. Rejection lasts a long time.

It suits everyone that people like Catherine Julien exist. They serve as bait for bullies. As long as Guillaume Piché is torturing Catherine Julien, he's leaving the others alone.

Guys like Guillaume Piché are raging tigers. In Grade 7, Catherine Julien tumbled into the beast's cage. We all witnessed her fall; we let it happen. For five years, she's been putting up with his attacks. During that time, the others have been free to live their lives. Catherine Julien plays an important role in my small private school.

At another table, Catherine Crosnier is eating her lunch with Catherine Bernier. Catherine Crosnier is the only person I have ever seen defend Catherine Julien. And she expects nothing in return. She keeps a low profile. She just goes about her business. I think I judged her wrongly. Deep down, she's maybe the least fake girl in the school.

Between two mouthfuls of ravioli, I ask Eugénie, "Are we rejects?"

"Who do you mean?"

"Us: you and me."

My friend rolls her eyes. "Who cares? We're getting the hell out of here in June."

I wasn't expecting that answer. "Eug, do you think we're rejects?"

She thinks about it. "We can't be rejects. There are two of us."

"Gangs of rejects exist."

"Sure, we're not popular. But I don't think we're rejects either. We're average. Normal."

Basically, we're the second-class passengers on the Titanic.

I cast a sidelong glance at Catherine Julien. The only time I ever really spoke to her was on the first day of high school, in September 1999, before everyone knew each other. Before the roles were assigned. Eventually, I understood that she'd landed the one of resident punching bag and that it was best to keep away from her.

"What was Catherine Julien like when you did your English project with her?"

Eugénie furrows her brow. "She was weird."

"Weird in what way?"

"She gets off on art history and Japan."

"Oh yeah . . ."

That *is* weird. "But you know, I get off on . . ."

My best friend stares at me, expressionless. "On what?"

"You know!"

"Say it, Colin!" She knows I won't say it. It amuses her to torture me like this. "Say it: You get off on Céline Dion."

"Shut up!"

I am seething inside. She doesn't know what my love for Céline represents, what it's liable to reveal about me.

"Relax, I have the right to say 'Céline Dion' at school. Anyway, no one heard."

Guillaume Piché walks past our table. I watch him out of the corner of my eye. He sits down across from Guillaume Langlois and Guillaume Arteau, two other popular stoners.

Eugénie, oblivious to danger, continues, "When you think of it, getting off on Céline Dion is almost as weird as getting off on art history and Japan."

“While you’re at it, you might as well just say it, so I can be a reject like Catherine Julien!”

“Come on, Colin. Catherine Julien could be anyone. She could be you or me. It’s just a question of luck.”

She’s not wrong. But an athletic blonde like Catherine Wagner or a tall, handsome, dark-haired guy like Guillaume Dionne could never have been members of the select club of rejects. Not at my little private school.

“Catherine Julien is just fine,” Eugénie concludes. “She’s nice and she has ideas. But she never had any luck.”

High school is a circus, a jungle, a zoo, one big, damn lottery.

50

BIG WHITE FACE SURROUNDED BY RED

LOOKING FOR A JOB is a nightmare for any sixteen-year-old.

First, you have to open a Word document, choose a pretty template, type without making mistakes and above all—above all—invent a life for yourself. Aptitudes. Skills. Interests. Passions. A personality. All those things you don't have.

Then, you have to put on your coat, your boots, leave the house, walk up to chemin Sainte-Foy, enter a random business and act like you want to work there. You have to be fake: smile politely, look sure of yourself, even when the cashier shoves the CV in a drawer and says she'll give it to her boss.

Next, when you don't hear from the boss, you have to listen to your parents suggest, "You should follow up with them. Call the store to say you're very interested in the position and would like a chance to show them what you can do. That always makes a difference with employers."

You have to reply that you'll do it, then not do it, then lie about it and swear you've done it. Then you have to repeat the whole process until you come across a manager who's desperate enough to hire an incompetent teenager on the spot.

When you finally land a job, you have to get up on Sunday morning to perform boring tasks under the supervision of a rigid adult. But as of that point, you're being paid, and therefore willing to put up with anything.

: :

I need money. Whether it's to go see Céline in Las Vegas or follow my boyfriend to Montreal, I have to work. I miss the knick-knack shop. Basically, I liked reigning over the displays of trinkets. I wonder if it would have closed if Manon Sirois hadn't died. Maybe I would have had a few more months to fill my bank account.

There's no school today—professional development day. With my parents and my brother out of the house, I go downstairs, update my CV and print three copies. Last summer, when I was trying to find a job, my parents urged me to hand out lots of CVs. Admittedly, at the time, my babysitting course was my only skill, and there was little chance of that impressing anyone. But, surprisingly, Manon Sirois immediately believed in me. I think she found me likeable. The knick-knack shop was only the third place I'd gone to.

Today, it will be the same thing: three CVs will be more than enough. I am not very ambitious. But after all, now I have my experience as a knick-knack salesperson under my belt.

Since I dream of taking the number 7 less often (it's always packed), I decide to only apply to businesses within walking distance. This considerably limits my options. My dream would be to work at the video store: I make it my first stop.

The woman behind the counter takes the CV that I hand her. "Do you have any experience?" she asks bluntly.

"I worked for seven months at a shop that just closed down."

"Which one?"

"The knick-knack shop across from Laval Hospital."

"Oh, it closed? Well . . ."

She looks at my CV, but I can tell she's not really reading it; she's thinking about what she wants to ask me.

"Do you know anything about movies?"

"A bit . . . I mean, quite a bit."

"If I said to you 'romantic comedy from the nineties starring Tom Hanks and Meg Ryan?'"

"*Sleepless in Seattle.*"

Easy. Céline sings the theme song.

"If I said to you 'Denys Arcand's latest film?'"

Does she take me for an idiot or what? Everyone knows that. "*Les Invasions barbares*."

"Who directed *Spirited Away*?"

No way. That's cheating if she starts asking me for the names of directors. Who walks into a video store looking for a certain director? People want film titles.

I pretend to rack my brain. "I used to know it . . . It's on the tip of my tongue . . ."

She is not impressed. She doesn't even bother to give me the answer.

"If I said 'science fiction movie from 2000 starring Jennifer Lopez?'"

I can picture the video cover. It's a big white face surrounded by red. I can picture it. What's the damn movie called? I toss out a title at random.

"*The Fifth Element*?"

The lady raises her eyebrows. She looks stunned. "Not even close. That's with Milla Jovovich. I was looking for *The Cell*. You know, the cover with the white face surrounded by red . . ."

Yes, I know, I remember! I should have described it to her, because that's what she ended up doing in any case. She thinks I'm useless. I'm ruining my chances of working here. I thought I was pretty good when I walked in here. But in the end, I know almost nothing.

"One last little one: a French film from 2003 with Charlotte Rampling and Ludivine Sagnier."

What! Charlotte who? Ludi what? Who would know that? That's a trick question. Better to remain silent than say something else stupid. I pretend to think while observing the woman. She has grey hair, a very smooth cut. Playmobil hair.

When I say nothing, the video store lady takes out a movie from under the counter: *Swimming Pool*! The bizarre, sexual film my parents rented the evening of Clément's birthday party, the evening I first set eyes on Yann's handsome face. This time, I'm the one who's stunned. I can't believe I missed that question. I want to explain that I know about that piece-of-shit movie, that I even saw a big chunk of it, but that would be pathetic, and she wouldn't believe me. In a weak voice, I try to defend myself.

"But I can always learn more about film . . . I love watching movies."

"Thank you, Colin. I'll think about it and let you know if I need you."

She won't ever call me. And from now on, I'll be embarrassed to rent my movies here.

: :

Women's clothing store: no. Asian restaurant: no. Christian radio station: no. I wind up at the pharmacy. The cashier goes to the back of the store and reappears with a mustachioed gentleman who frowns at me. He doesn't touch the CV that I dropped on the cash.

"How old are you?" he asks.

"Sixteen."

"What's your availability?"

"Every Sunday."

He recoils slightly. "Just Sundays? I need more hours than that from you."

This guy is dreaming in colour. "It's because I'm in high school, sir."

He suddenly seems to find me very difficult. "Okay, look, I don't think this is going to work out, let's stop here . . . Good luck in your endeavours."

And he walks off toward the back of the store. The cashier gives me a meaningful look. I feel like I've had a narrow escape. That man seemed moderately crazy.

::

I walk past another restaurant, the gas station, the florist, the bakery and the grocery store. I'm now more than a ten-minute walk from home. That's my limit. I don't want to work far away. But I still have one CV. It would be dumb not to get rid of it. Dropping off only two CVs is a bit silly. Three is already better.

I enter a dog grooming salon. The woman greets me with a radiant expression and a big smile. She consults my CV.

"Do you have experience with animals?"

"Not really . . ."

"Have you ever had pets?"

"No, not really . . ."

"Are you in regular contact with animals?"

"Sometimes . . ."

The woman's expression sours a bit more with each answer I give. What am I doing here? I have made another bad decision.

I shrug. "But I really like dogs," I say, as if that were enough.

In reality, I'm scared stiff of big dogs. As for the little ones, they bark all the time, and it gets on my nerves.

"Oh yes, you like dogs?"

My argument does not convince her. Now she's doubting me. She kindly explains, "To work here, you have to be very comfortable around dogs. Dogs can sense our fear and discomfort. It makes them nervous. Which is the opposite of what we want to do. They come here for a relaxing experience. Do you understand? I think you should apply elsewhere."

And she hands me back my CV. No! A CV is something you give, not something you take back. I back up toward the shop door.

"Just keep it. Maybe you'll need me. You never know."

I leave quickly. Mission accomplished: I dropped off three CVs. The rest of the day belongs to me.

And that's how you look for a job when you're sixteen years old.

::

Back from my rounds, I log on to MSN to complain to Yann Moreau:

My CV is ridiculous and I don't
know how to sell myself.
Him: *Don't get discouraged, handsome.*
I believe in you.:)

I'm not used to someone calling me "handsome." He even seems to think it. At the knick-knack shop, Manon Sirois often called me "beautiful," but it had nothing to do with my body. It was just her way of asking me to dust the frog trinkets.

51

A VAST TERRITORY

EUGÉNIE HAS JUST LEFT. We spent the evening laughing in my room. When we talk like that for hours, I feel blessed. I relish how lucky I am. Our friendship is enough to occupy us. We always have something to say to each other.

My stereo system was playing a mix tape of Céline songs that are hard to find on CD. Few people like to listen to Céline Dion's voice as much as me, though Eugénie never asks me to play something else. Yet this evening, during "Ma chambre," she said, "Can I ask you a question?"

As if she needed to forewarn me.

"You just have."

She continued, "Do you ever listen to other music?"

Normally, this type of cross-examination gets on my nerves. But this evening, a perfect evening of laughter and shared moments, nothing could aggravate me.

"Of course, come on," I said at first. "I listen to the radio, I listen to my parents' music and my brother's . . ."

"I know, but are there other artists that you like? That you *really* like?"

Eugénie likes Destiny's Child, Christina Aguilera, Pink, Dido, Jean Leloup and Projet Orange. Her tastes are diversified. She even had an Evanescence phase, but that's behind her.

I knew she wouldn't judge me, but I gave her a dishonest answer just the same. "I'm just in a Céline Dion phase."

"Since . . ."

"Since 1996."

"At this point, it's not just a phase. It's your entire musical world."

She was right. Céline is my world.

Seen from the outside, it's a narrow world. A very small space. Yet, for me, her music covers a vast territory. With Céline, there is a song for every mood and every occasion. Her discography is a shopping centre; it's Place Laurier. Radiohead is Place Ste-Foy. Björk is the knick-knack shop: meant for a niche audience, really not for everyone. Yann would find it terrible to compare an artist's work to a shop. Not me. I always have a good time at Place Laurier.

I know Céline Dion's face better than my own. When I see her in a magazine or on TV, my heart soars a little, just like when I run into Eugénie walking around the neighbourhood. Céline's face is the incarnation of her voice.

The uniqueness of my situation does not escape me. If I were to survey the students in my high school, a crushing majority would claim they never listen to Céline Dion. I would become a first-class reject. The Catherine Julien of musical preferences.

52
THE DAMNED 13

THIS MORNING, the sky fell on my parents' heads. They received a phone call and flew into an angry panic.

"Jesus Christ . . ."

When my father swears, it's serious. I finally manage to understand, through their annoyed explanations, that Matante Pauline has had a heart attack and was rushed to hospital. Of course, it falls to my mother, her niece, to take charge of everything. She is very unhappy about this. It stresses her out. It isn't that she doesn't love her aunt, but it's one more responsibility. It's too much.

The bad news has ruined their appetites. They throw out the rest of their cereal and go to their room to get dressed.

"At least she lives across from Saint-Sacrement Hospital," I hear my father say.

"So what?" my mother replies.

"Well, I don't know. The ambulance must have gotten there quickly. They took care of her right away."

Clément doesn't seem overly disturbed. Nothing really bothers my brother. He has the capacity for surprise of a cactus. My parents reappear in the kitchen, ready to leave. My mother looks at me. "Nice start to a Saturday, eh?" she says.

A big crease marks her forehead. I shrug. What am I supposed to do? Initiative is not my finest quality. But I ask all the same, fingers crossed under the table. "Do you want me to come with you?"

"No, no. No, thank you. We'll fill you in later."

Phew.

: :

Since I have nothing to do with the crisis that's worrying my parents, I suggest to Eugénie that we spend the day at Place Laurier. We meet up at rue Lavallée, at the stop for the 13. It snowed all night. It's blindingly white outside.

The bus is supposed to come by at 11:22. So we wait. And wait. And wait some more. At 11:34, still nothing in sight! It's not that serious; we have so much to tell each other.

At 11:46, it becomes clear that the bus is not going to show. On Saturdays, the 13 passes only once an hour. Do we wait another half-hour, hoping the 12:22 bus shows up on schedule? Or would it be better to head to the 800 bus stop, fifteen minutes' walk away?

I'm fuming. Eugénie couldn't care less.

"Calm down, it's just a bus. We'll just walk to the 800."

"It's not that; it's the principle! I can't take it, the damned 13 that only shows up half the time. It's the only bus in our neighbourhood, and it only comes when it feels like it."

"It's because of the snow. It must be stuck somewhere." My friend pulls me by the arm.

"I don't feel like climbing back up the entire hill to catch the 800!" I whine.

"Colin, you live at the top of the hill anyway. Come on!"

I feel like I've been taken hostage by my city's defective public transportation system. It's awful. Then I remember that Matante Pauline is in the hospital for a heart attack. I shut my yap and follow Eugénie to the 800 stop.

: :

When we return from the shopping centre in the late afternoon, Marie-Louise and Daniel still aren't back. The only ones home are Clément and his Catherine Moreau of a girlfriend, who are fooling around in the living room.

"Have you heard from our parents?" I ask my brother.

"No."

His girlfriend stares at Eugénie intensely. "Are you two dating?" she asks.

I roll my eyes. This idiotic question has been following us around since grade school. "No, we're just friends," I reply coldly. "What's for dinner?"

Clément stares at me like I was alighting from a flying saucer. "Do I know? I'm not Mom."

"Is Catherine having dinner here?"

"Yes."

Well, if my brother's girlfriend can stay for dinner, so can my best friend. My parents will no doubt be home soon. It's not their style to leave us hanging.

: :

On their way back from the hospital, Marie-Louise and Daniel stopped at Ashton. They come into the house, exhausted, arms filled with delicious-smelling paper bags. They didn't know Eugénie would be here, but it doesn't matter: the poutines are so big that they'll be enough.

At dinner, I'm anxious to know everything. "How is Matante Pauline?"

My mother motions to my father to answer; she has clearly had enough.

"She's doing well, she'll recover. But she wants to move into a residence. She doesn't want to go back to the Samuel Holland. She says she needs a place with services. We also met with a social worker who completely agreed."

No one reacts.

“Oh! That’s good . . .” Eugénie ventures. “She’ll be better off that way. You must be pleased . . .”

My mother nods and smiles at my best friend, as if to say, “You poor innocent thing.”

“It’ll be a huge job to move her,” my father explains. “Her apartment is full of stuff. Full, full of stuff. We’ll have to sort through it all. She’s always had trouble getting rid of things. She’s a hoarder.”

Marie-Louise inhales deeply. “Okay, can we talk about something else? Let’s talk about something else! Eugénie, how is your mother?”

My parents’ stress is palpable. A new problem has crept into their lives. Clément and Catherine Moreau are whispering sweet nothings to one another like nothing out of the ordinary was just said. A moment later, they get up and go down to the basement. Those two live in a carefree bubble. If I had the opportunity to love Yann Moreau out in the open, I could forget about all my cares, too, and focus solely on the desire I feel for him. Instead of that, I think about Matante Pauline’s poor health.

53

FAREWELL PRESENT

SINCE JANUARY, in gym class, we have been playing volleyball. I don't understand why it's taken five years for the teacher to introduce it. We've done basketball and soccer every year, badminton, and even rugby in the snow.

Since it is a very exotic sport, there is no volleyball team at my small private school. Everyone is bad at this sport. Everyone sucks, as my brother would say. Even Guillaume Dionne, even Catherine Laramée. Everyone is lousy at it. It's wonderful.

First, no one can serve overhand like the real volleyball players. So everyone does it underhand, which makes for very slow serves. The person in the path of the ball has all the time in the world to try for a bump. Then, if by some miracle, their bump is successful and the ball remains in play, a second person has to be willing to set the ball so that, finally, a third person can try to send it over the net. Since all the students are uniformly lousy, that person has absolutely no pressure. They hit the ball however they please, and it either veers off dramatically and hits the net or falls outside the court. Everyone bitches at everyone else; everyone is in a bad mood—except me—then we start over again. It's extremely democratic. Finally, a sport that is just my style.

Last week, I spent the entire class standing at the back of the court without touching the ball once. I had to pinch myself; I thought I was dreaming. It's like high school is giving me a little farewell present.

54

FRACTURED SKULL

MY PARENTS ARE COMPLETELY OVERWHELMED by what has happened. It's the third Saturday in a row that they've gone to Matante Pauline's apartment to help her clean up and pack boxes. But she's having trouble throwing out her trinkets. My father says she clings to even the smallest newspaper clipping. It's an impossible task. Daniel and Marie-Louise have gotten caught in the bric-a-brac trap of the Samuel Holland. Never could I have imagined, when I was selling knick-knacks to the old ladies of Quebec City, that I was contributing to cluttering their homes.

Oddly, this situation is working to my advantage: over the past two weeks, my romantic relationship has kicked into second gear. On Saturday, as soon as Clément leaves to meet his girlfriend at her place, I invite Yann Moreau over. And we spend the whole afternoon together. In my room. In my bed. It turns him on like crazy, and me too. The first time we made love at my place, I banged my head against the wall and almost fractured my skull.

The second time, we dared to walk around the house nude. It was exhilarating. When I told Eugénie, she told me we were playing with fire. As usual, she was right. We are becoming reckless. But it's so good!

The third time, Yann brought his Radiohead albums, and we turned up the volume until the living room speakers vibrated. The music was like a shelter for us. We kissed for hours without thinking about anything else.

Each time we part, he takes my face between his hands and says *I love you,* exactly like on Christmas Eve at Sainte-Geneviève Park. Yann Moreau and I will never break up.

55

LOOKING LIKE A FLOOZIE

IN PLACE LAURIER there is a store that sells a wide selection of evening wear for short teenagers like Eugénie: Laura Petites. That's where my best friend asks me to go with her and her mother to find her prom dress.

It's quite something to go shopping for expensive clothing. My mother and I bought my prom suit last week, at Tristan & America, and I couldn't believe the amount she was willing to spend on clothes I'll practically never wear again. Taking out her credit card, she said, "You can wear the shirt again at Christmas, it's classic. The pants, too."

I had chosen a simple, elegant design: "timeless appeal," the salesman had said. Prom isn't all that exciting for me: at best, it's a moderately entertaining evening, the outcome of five years in social limbo; at worst, it's the grand finale of the painful power dynamics of high school.

::

Liette, Eugénie's mother, is dragging her feet in the shopping centre. She is a sociable lady who walks horribly slowly and sometimes stops to chat with strangers; even in grade school I could outpace her without any effort. But her attitude changes the minute we walk into Laura Petites. She abruptly calls over a young saleswoman.

"Miss, my daughter is looking for a dress for her prom; she wants something long, but not low-cut, flared at the bottom, black with sparkles. Do you have that?"

What's gotten into her? I have never seen her so stressed. Especially since Eugénie never said exactly what style of dress she wanted. My friend gives me a shocked look.

"The prom dresses are over there . . ." the saleswoman says very softly.

A vague gesture accompanies her reply. Eugénie and I rush over to the racks filled with dozens of dresses in all colours. I like all the models; they all look elegant, sparkly. It's the opposite of a men's department, where you feel like you're choosing a suit to be buried in. But my best friend and her mother are more critical; they rummage around for a long time, then Eugénie ends up pulling out a red satin dress. "This one, Mom."

Liette tilts her head to one side and twists her mouth to the other. "I don't know, sweetheart . . . You can always try it on, but . . ."

Really not encouraging.

Eugénie, who knows how to stand up to her parents, nevertheless disappears into the fitting room. While she is changing, Liette takes me aside.

"Do you like that dress?" she whispers. "I don't think it's her style. I think she's going to look like a . . . a . . . I think she'll be laughed at if she wears that. Prom is important . . . What about you, do you like the dress? What do you think? Tell her what you think, Colin, she'll listen to you. You have good taste; she'll listen to you."

Stunned by her panic, I shrug my shoulders. Liette returns to rummage through the displays. She frantically pushes away big tulle crinolines, breathing heavily. I don't recognize the affable, laughing mother of my friend. She has become another woman. The speakers in the shop are playing "La neige au Sahara" by Anggun. Everything is upside down.

The fitting room curtain slides open, and Eugénie reappears. A shiver runs through my entire body. She is magnificent. She walks toward the mirror, turns around, and admires herself for a moment. "So? Do you like it?"

Her beauty takes my breath away. "It's superb. It's perfect. You're perfect."

In the mirror my friend flashes me a huge smile. She's so pretty, so cool, Eugénie Bujold.

Liette, her head still tilted, says, "But you can't try on just one, my dear. You have to try on at least three, see what you like, what suits you."

"I like it, it suits me. It does suit me, eh, Colin?"

I nod emphatically. "It fits you like a glove." I've always wanted to say that to someone.

The young saleswoman, who has kept to the background since we arrived, approaches and cries, "Oh! It's like it was made for you. That red goes so well with your complexion! Rich, warm, deep. I call it Bergman red. An excellent choice."

Liette gets a bit annoyed. "But she's going to try a few others before making her decision."

"No, this is the one I want."

"Look, dear, I found others that would look good on you . . ." She points to two black dresses that she found on the racks.

"No, I'm sure. I love it. Colin loves it, too, and so does the saleswoman. You don't like it, Mom?"

Eugénie's mother places both hands on her chin. "I don't know, dear . . . I really don't know . . . Maybe we should show it to your father before . . . I don't know what your father would think of a long red dress like that . . . You're not afraid you'll look . . . like a floozie?"

Immediately, the saleswoman backs up toward her cash. She wants nothing to do with this weird exchange. I envy her for being able to beat a retreat.

My best friend stares at me in the mirror, her mouth wide open. Her sweet mom has turned into the puritanical policewoman of prom dresses. Eugénie is fuming.

"No, Liette, I'm not afraid of looking like a floozie in my long dress from Laura Petites."

She returns to the fitting room, changes in a flash, comes back out and doesn't say another word.

The car ride home seems to take three hours. Eugénie sits in the back, next to me, and holds my hand, glassy-eyed.

::

Her: *So my father told my mother not to buy a floozie dress. Like he's scared it's going to make me sleep with a guy. He just realized I'm not eight years old anymore, the dumbass. And my mother is so easily influenced, she does everything he says anyway. Like, do they think I'm going to get raped just because I'm wearing a red dress?*

Her: *What a stupid family!*

Sitting in front of the basement computer, I could not agree more with my best friend. Maybe Eugénie and I are finally reaching that point in life where we know more than our parents, where our parents can no longer see clearly. Does a girl who chooses to wear a red dress have to be on her guard? It won't make Eugénie feel very good, going to the prom with that kind of doubt in her heart. I never dreamed that a shopping trip would lead to such drama. I had no idea that inside that handsome man who works at Desjardins lay a controlling father worried about a Laura Petites dress. He's acting like Eugénie went shopping at the sex shop on rue Bouvier. Yet Michel Bujold strolls around in his sexy undies in front of his daughter's best friend without the slightest fear of being raped.

Her: *I want to run away.*
Me: *Don't do that! Call the Kids Help Phone!;)*
Her: *LOL*

Silence, then she concludes:

I will have that damned red dress.

I don't even doubt it. Nothing stops that girl.

56

IT DOESN'T COUNT

TEN DAYS AGO, Guillaume Arteau started talking about a big party he was planning to throw at his place. His parents were going to New York for the whole weekend. He had to take advantage.

I've never liked Guillaume Arteau, and I'm sure he couldn't care less about me. In five years, he must have spoken to me three times. But it's already spring; it's the end of high school, and it seems like things are changing. All the Grade 11 students were invited to Guillaume Arteau's party. *Every single one.* Even me. Even Catherine Julien. At least, I think so.

"Are you going?" Eugénie asks me.

I lob the question back to my best friend. "Are *you* going?"

She shrugs. Eugénie and I have been thrown off balance. This is the first time someone has ever smashed down social barriers like this. Of course, it had to come from the top, from one of the five or six alpha guys at school. Or else it never would have worked. At least, I don't think so. I'm no longer sure of anything.

: :

On Saturday, April 3, 2004, at eight o'clock in the evening, Eugénie and I arrive at Guillaume Arteau's house. Already present are: Catherine Laramée, Catherine Wagner, Catherine Pronovost, Catherine Crosnier, Catherine Bernier, Catherine Lopez, Catherine Doré, Catherine Perry, Catherine Ryan, Catherine Marquette, Catherine Richard, Catherine Drouin, Catherine Lefebvre, Catherine Dubois, Catherine Joly, Catherine Fecteau, Catherine Bélanger, Catherine Tremblay, Catherine Gagnon, Catherine Laporte, Catherine Dubé, Catherine Mathieu, Catherine Bédard, Catherine Corbeil, Catherine Papillon, Catherine Gignac, Catherine Boisclair, Catherine Beauregard, Catherine Martin, Catherine Lévesque; Guillaume Dionne, Guillaume Piché, Guillaume Langlois, Guillaume Brassard, Guillaume Paré, Guillaume Côté, Guillaume Racine, Guillaume Caramagno, Guillaume Jobin, Guillaume Langevin, Guillaume Buteau, Guillaume Delamarre, Guillaume Gauthier, Guillaume Gendron, Guillaume Beaulieu, Guillaume Verreau, Guillaume Farinaccio, Guillaume Bérard, Guillaume Hervé, Guillaume Dumais, Guillaume Riverin, Guillaume Lessard, Guillaume Godin, Guillaume Ouimet, Guillaume Fortier.

All these people gathered together in a bungalow in Cap-Rouge is a phenomenon I'm having trouble grasping.

No Catherine Julien in sight. Either Guillaume Arteau didn't invite her, or she decided to stay home. Maybe she told herself there are limits to being bullied outside of school hours. She isn't wrong. On the weekend, everyone should have the right to lead a life free from bullying.

::

Everyone has a can or a bottle in their hand. There is alcohol everywhere. I don't know where it's coming from; I didn't bring any. Aside from a few sips of my father's Budweiser, I have never drunk alcohol. Eugénie, more resourceful than I, hands me an ice-cold bottle: Smirnoff Ice. I remove the cap and moisten my lips. It tastes like polar shit. I walk around the house regularly pretending to take sips.

In the living room, an adult sound system is playing party songs very loudly: "Blue (Da Ba Dee)," "Hey Ya!," "Crazy in Love," "Yeah!," "Lady Marmalade," "Shut Up," "Cry Me a River," "The Real Slim Shady" . . . A few confident girls dance together while Guillaume Langlois and Guillaume Piché watch them from a distance.

Then Catherine Wagner appears from the kitchen, looking rather excited, thank you very much, reaches into her bag, and takes out a CD that she inserts in the player. I recognized the case: the Spice Girls' first album. Catherine Wagner turns the volume dial. The house shakes.

Yo, I'll tell you what I want,
what I really, really want
So tell me what you want,
what you really, really want
I'll tell you what I want,
what I really, really want
So tell me what you want,
what you really, really want
I wanna, I wanna, I wanna, I wanna,
I wanna really, really, really wanna zigazig-ah

Instantly, cries ring out from every room, and a swarm of students descends on the living room. Catherine Pronovost brushes past us, shouting, "This song reminds me so much of elementary school!"

Eugénie pulls me into the middle of the group. Everyone is jumping around, even me, shouting the words to "Wannabe." I quiver with pleasure. This hymn is irresistible.

The ecstasy is maintained during "Say You'll Be There," then comes "2 Become 1," a slow song. I was not prepared to slow dance. I'm pulled back to earth and glance around me. Catherine Wagner,

Catherine Pronovost, Catherine Bernier, Catherine Dubé, Catherine Papillon, Catherine Boisclair, Catherine Lopez, Catherine Doré, Catherine Gagnon, Catherine Beauregard, Catherine Dubois, Catherine Lefebvre, Catherine Joly, Catherine Fecteau. Eugénie Bujold. And me, Colin Bourque. Alone in the middle of the girls.

Several guys, beer in hand, are standing on the edge of the dance floor. None of them has answered the call of Ginger, Scary, Baby, Sporty and Posh. All that time, they just stood there watching us dance, me and the girls, to the Spice Girls. I can see the mocking sneers on their faces. I shouldn't have been there. It wasn't my place. I let down my guard. Burning with shame, I escape discreetly to the bathroom, where I pour my entire bottle of Smirnoff Ice down the sink.

::

In the living room, Eugénie is still shaking it with the girls. I find myself alone, and it bothers me, but I can see she's having fun. She's not my babysitter.

I push through the mass of drunken teenagers in the kitchen and go downstairs, where there's a completely different atmosphere. There's no music here, aside from a few conversations punctuated by coarse laughter. The fluorescent ceiling lights blind me.

In one corner, Catherine Crosnier is talking to Guillaume Brassard. After Eugénie, Catherine Crosnier is the person I know best here, so I head toward her, but Guillaume Brassard raises his hand and caresses her shoulder. Stunned, I freeze. I can't join them now. They're flirting with each other; I'd be interrupting. Oh no, are they about to kiss? I imagine them having sex, then my mind is flooded with the image of my boyfriend's naked body, which I drive away so I don't get hard in Guillaume Arteau's overly bright basement.

Catherine Laramée, whom I hadn't noticed nearby, claps her hands and announces, "Okay, guys, we're gonna play a game!"

Shit.

The dozen people present gather in the middle of the room. Catherine Laramée drains the rest of her Boomerang, which she brandishes above her head like a trophy.

"Let's play spin the bottle!" she declares.

Oh, fuck!

At this party, I'm definitely the person *no one* wants to kiss. I look awful, I have no sex appeal, and I'm an enigma to the others.

But I can't sneak out: everyone would see me, I'd look like a wimp. Damned fluorescent bungalow basement lights. Paradoxically, the fluorescent bungalow basement lights are the best possible lighting for spin the bottle. Because it really is just a show. Everyone wants to see the tip of the tongue slide into the half-open mouth; everyone wants to play voyeur to other people's discomfort. While waiting to put on a show themselves.

Personally, I'm so uncomfortable, I'm paralyzed. I've sat down on the floor, as far back as possible, but still in the circle of players, unwillingly. My arms are wrapped around my knees; my posture gives off a degree of hostility, but after all, that's what I am—hostile, dammit.

The bottle spins: Catherine Laramée and Guillaume Gauthier. A timid kiss, mouth closed. It's the beginning of the game; nervous laughter.

The bottle spins: Catherine Corbeil and Guillaume Caramagno. A sensual kiss, soft lips. I force myself to smile like the others.

The bottle spins: Guillaume Lessard and Catherine Fecteau. A slimy French kiss, endless. I'm open-mouthed. Some people have no shame.

The bottle spins: Guillaume Dionne and Guillaume Brassard. The best athlete in the school and the handsome nerd from Group B. The Boomerang has spoken. They must comply, must follow the rules. No cheating allowed. I'm breathless. A bottle has spun, and two boys are about to kiss in front of me.

The whole group bursts out laughing. Cries, jeers, jibes, elbowing, thigh-slapping. Guillaume Brassard is not laughing. He looks at Guillaume Dionne, who's staring at the floor.

Without looking up, Dionne says, "Well, you have to spin again. That doesn't count."

Guillaume Brassard doesn't move. He almost seems to be waiting for our permission. Catherine Laramée shouts, "No way, you have to kiss! Come on! It's the game!"

The two Guillaumes stare at one another intensely, like Yann and me before our first kiss, on Christmas Eve. They aren't really going to . . . Is there a chance they'll . . .?

No. Of course not. It was just me projecting. Guillaume Dionne grabs the bottle, slams it down in front of Guillaume Brassard and exclaims violently, "Christ, you're disgusting! What are you waiting for, man? Come on, spin the bottle! Are you gay or what?"

Finally, Guillaume Brassard complies. Everyone, led by Catherine Laramée, boos the two players. I take advantage to slip away.

Upstairs, I find my coat, tell Eugénie I'm leaving and go wait for the bus on the corner.

It's spring; it's the end of high school, but nothing has really changed.

57
DONNACONA

THE DAY AFTER GUILLAUME ARTEAU'S PARTY, I need love.

My parents are at Matante Pauline's for their "last Sunday of decluttering before the move," as they promised me hopefully before leaving. Because next week Matante Pauline is leaving her apartment. She's found a seniors' residence nearby, in the Saint-Sacrement neighbourhood. It makes sense: the old people at the Samuel Holland need somewhere to go afterward.

Clément has borrowed my mother's car to take his girlfriend to Trois-Rivières. I don't have the slightest idea what they'll do there. Trois-Rivières seems to have little to offer two young lovebirds. Especially compared to Quebec City.

Like I've done every Sunday for a month, I invite my boyfriend over to spend the day in my bed.

::

Yann Moreau is making fun of me.

"Come on, handsome, did you really think they were going to make out?"

“How would I know? It was my first time playing spin the bottle.”

He pulls me toward him, covers our heads with the sheet and grabs my butt. That’s his favourite part of my body.

“Anyway, I got the hell out after that. I didn’t even get drunk. I’m really not a party guy.”

He kisses me. “Maybe that party was really not for you.”

“Maybe. Too bad. Fuck it.” My indifference is feigned.

Yann stretches out over me. Our naked bodies quiver. I wrap my legs around his body; he arches his back; I feel the warmth of his penis against mine. I forget everything—I surrender control to him.

: :

Freezing rain is falling. On the sidewalk outside my house, passersby move at a snail’s pace. Crouching near the front door, Yann puts on his boots to head home. Barefoot, my head in the clouds, I caress his hair.

Outside, a car door slams. Followed by another. I brace myself, panicking. My parents, already? Clément and his girlfriend, already? I’m practically having a heart attack.

Yann Moreau raises a resigned face to me. No, Yann. No! This is not the time. The right time hasn't come. I'm not ready. I'm not seventeen yet; I'm not prepared. I don't have enough time. There is no time, only stolen time, fear, disaster ahead.

The door opens. It's Clément and Catherine Moreau, who exclaim in unison, "Yann?"

"Hello!" my boyfriend says.

For once, my brother looks surprised. It's taken all these years for me to discover what his face looks like when he changes expressions. "What are you doing here?" he cries.

Immediately, Yann Moreau replies, "Well, I came to see you, C. But you weren't here. So I was leaving."

His reply chills me to the bone. Bad answer. Not believable. Yann may well be on the same swim team as my brother, but he is not one of his best friends. I'd never seen him at our place before Clément's birthday party.

But my brother is an uncomplicated person; it's immediately clear that he believes Yann and is ready to move on to something else. His girlfriend, on the other hand, doesn't let it go.

"Why did you take off your boots, then?"

My boyfriend cleverly plays the annoyed brother card—good strategy; it's also what I would have done. "Leave me alone, Cat, dammit. I needed to piss. I went. Now I'm leaving. Is that okay, Agatha Christie?"

Catherine Moreau still looks puzzled.

Clément is already in the kitchen, a cookie in his mouth. "We didn't make it to Trois-Rivières, the 40 was too icy. We went to Donnacona instead."

Jesus, Donnacona. It's worse than Trois-Rivières. What on earth could they have done there all day?

My brother concludes, "Anyway, that's that. I have to go take a crap. Bye, Yann! See you at college."

My secret love leaves the house without a glance at me.

I rush to my room: the bed is unmade; there's a bunch of Kleenex on the floor; it reeks of sex. I have just enough time to slam the door before Catherine Moreau, my brother's girlfriend, my boyfriend's sister, walks past it. She didn't see anything. At least I don't think so.

58

BELLA GOTH

THE MORE TIME PASSES, the more I'm becoming obsessed with the truth. Yet I'm perpetuating a great lie that is slowly swallowing me up, without stopping, like quicksand. One day, I hope more than I sense, something will change, and I'll change, too. For the moment, it would take the threat of a nuclear winter to make me talk.

I've taken out *The Sims* again, a computer game that simulates real life. You have to control a human being, build them a house, make them earn money, meet other Sims, find love, build a family . . . I've been spending a lot of time on it the past few weeks. It's my new occupation, a very tidy, ordered reality.

My Sim, named Elisabeth Courval, has a little blob of blonde hair and a long, multicoloured dress. At first, she worked as a golf caddy, but as soon as I had the money to buy her a piano, I got her a gig as a subway musician, because in this game, a musician earns much more than a slacker.

Elisabeth Courval has worked her way up: she's now a rock star. She rakes in one thousand four hundred Simoleans a day. But to get the ultimate promotion (record producer), she needs fifteen friends. In *The Sims,* a large pool of friends is needed for career advancement. Fortunately, it's only a game. If it were like that in real life, I'd be doomed to rot at the bottom of the ladder forever.

Elisabeth is stagnating at fourteen friends. In order not to lose them, she must maintain her friendships. As soon as she gets home from work, she entertains one or two Sims at home. She then spends part of the evening conversing with them to boost their relationship meter. Then she sends everyone home, eats dinner, watches a bit of TV and goes to bed. The next day, it starts over. Fourteen friends are a lot. It's already too many.

Despite everything, I'm determined to have another Sim enter her life who will become both the fifteenth friend and the husband. I try desperately to invite Mortimer Goth over, the neighbour across the street, to lure him away from his wife, Bella. But he refuses three-quarters of the time, and when he ends up coming over, he gets angry. I think his zodiac sign (Taurus) and my Sim's (Virgo) are incompatible. On the other hand, Bella Goth (Cancer) doesn't wait for an invitation to show up; she rings the bell three times a day. Yesterday, I wanted to do a few renovations, and she just stood in the middle of the yard, right where I was trying to dig a pool. Bella Goth is useless!

::

Elisabeth Courval is falling in love with Bella Goth. After seeing her pop up again and again, I ended up letting Bella in, and now the two women get along beautifully. This evening, they started flirting with each other. There's a kiss in the near future. With her little red dress and femme-fatale look, Bella Goth sets hearts reeling everywhere she goes.

That's not what I'd intended for my Sim; it isn't what I'd wanted. She was supposed to marry Mortimer Goth and have two children. Elisabeth Courval escapes me. I have no control, even over her. If it keeps on like this, I'm going to drown her in her pool, destroy the house and start all over again.

59
"PRIÈRE PAÏENNE"

MY PARENTS HAVE RECEIVED AN INVITATION to the baptism of Ghislaine Baril's daughter's baby, and I've decided to go with them, to convince myself that I am evolving, progressing, that the thought of a celebration filled with strangers no longer terrifies me like before. Clément, of course, expresses no interest in the event. He's happy to have the house to himself so he can screw around with his girlfriend.

I put on my prom shirt and pants. Marie-Louise is delighted: She's getting a return on her investment. I look like a little gentleman decked out like this. My father whistles when I walk by, the dumbass. My mother laughs.

"Daniel, you're so silly!"

There's a good mood throughout the house. The month of May is off to a good start.

::

My father takes the wheel. When a lady is alone in a car, she has no choice but to drive. But as soon as there's a man in the car, he's the one who drives. I never understood why, but that's how it is.

It's like my parents want to make me happy; they've put on Céline's album *1 fille & 4 types* in the car's CD player. They give a running commentary on each song. My mother really likes "Tout l'or des hommes" and "Contre nature"; my father prefers "Et je t'aime encore" and "Retiens-moi." I listen attentively, rediscovering the album from their point of view. The moment is both awkward and thrilling. Basically, all I ever want is their approval. I get it at unexpected moments, in ways they maybe don't even realize.

When the CD ends, my mother turns on the radio and, randomly, "Prière païenne" is playing.

"You're so lucky, my prince, it's like Céline is following you!"

Marie-Louise and Daniel giggle. Everyone likes "Prière païenne."

::

The church is magnificent.

"Small villages always have the nicest churches," my mother declares.

In Sainte-Foy, they're all modern and ugly; the one in our parish is the least objectionable.

The place is packed because they are blessing several babies at the same time. We find a pew in the back. I can't really see what's happening; I don't understand very much of the ceremony. I look at the stained glass windows and the statues. Who still baptizes their child in 2004? I stand when my parents stand, sit at the same time as they do. They're old enough to know exactly what to do during a mass. Right in the middle of a moment of contemplation, a man sneezes loudly in the church, startling everyone. We even hear Ghislaine Baril exclaim, "Good lord!"

Then comes the dreaded moment when the priest orders us to shake the hand of the other Christians in the congregation. The stranger in the next pew turns to me and extends his old fingers. I escape by taking a Kleenex out of my pocket to blow my nose loudly. My father isn't fooled by my manoeuvre and sighs. He thinks I'm unsociable and rude. I don't give a damn. There are limits to being extroverted.

::

At the reception following the baptism, at Ghislaine Baril's house, there's a feast. My mother's friend has prepared a buffet worthy of the finest caterers: chicken, egg, and ham sandwiches; coleslaw; potato salad; macaroni salad; tons of veggies and various dips; little cubes of marble cheddar; bunches of grapes; sweet pickles; pickled onions; olives. Sugar pie, Rice Krispies squares and brownies for dessert. I think of Eugénie, huge fan of cold lunches, who would love this.

I go back for thirds. I keep my mouth full to avoid making conversation. It works—they almost leave me alone. But I eat so much that I end up with a stomach ache. Here comes the diarrhea. Not ideal in a house full of strangers. I rush to the basement so I can go in peace. Everything comes out in seconds. I wipe quickly and go back upstairs, no one the wiser.

But at the top of the stairs, I come across one of Ghislaine Baril's twins, the mother of the newly Catholic baby. I can't avoid her.

"He did well, your Guillaume!"

She is still holding her belly like when she was pregnant. "He did well, eh?"

"He didn't even cry!" I reply.

She nods. A teenager walks behind her. Since I've run out of things to say, I ask, "Is that the father?"

"No, that's not him," she says. "The father isn't here."

"Where is he?"

"In Abitibi."

"How's that?"

The words come out of my mouth on their own. Embarrassment always makes me run at the mouth. The young mother starts to look uncomfortable, and she has every right to be; I am not minding my own business.

"He's had a guys' trip planned for a long time. He couldn't cancel."

"Oh, that's all right!" I say, in a falsely warm voice.

Since she adds nothing further to this stupid conclusion, I return to the kitchen to scrape the bottom of the potato salad bowl.

: :

On the way home, the sky darkens, and it starts to rain as we're crossing the Pierre-Laporte Bridge. My mother is talking about how the baby's father wasn't even there for the birth and how his attitude has really upset Ghislaine Baril.

"It's driving her crazy. She's picturing having to raise her grandson, at almost fifty years old . . . I tried consoling her, told her maybe he'd get used to the idea and step up, but that would honestly surprise me. He just took off, the bum."

Without even thinking, because it's really second nature for me, I challenge her. "Why did you tell her that if you don't believe it?"

Marie-Louise doesn't answer. Daniel, his eyes still focused on the road, says, "What? Because you never lie, Colin?"

My mother turns toward me to catch my reaction. I huddle in the corner of the seat to avoid meeting her eyes. My own lie is silence; she must know that.

60

PEAR JUICE

"I'M BORED."

Marie-Louise, seated on the other side of the living room, hands me a book. "Read this. I just finished it, it's excellent."

Memoirs of Hadrian, by Marguerite Yourcenar. A hefty tome. Do I look like I want to do homework on a Sunday? I am not that desperate.

"It takes place in Roman times."

"That's supposed to convince me?"

My mother sighs. "Go see Matante Pauline at her residence, then. She hasn't seen you since Christmas, she'd love a visit from you . . ."

My heart skips a beat. I should have kept my big mouth shut. Why do I always have to complain? Casually, Marie-Louise has set a trap that is now closing in on me; she has sown the seed of guilt. The Earth will not stop turning if I refuse to visit Matante Pauline, but a cruel image will darken the rest of my day, my week even: that of an old lady sitting alone in front of her television, her face as long as a fiddle.

"Say hi from me," my mother quips, as if reading my mind.

::

If I always thought the Samuel Holland looked like an old folks' home, it's because I'd never set foot in a real seniors' residence. At the Manoir Saint-Sacrement, Matante Pauline's new home, everyone looks noticeably older and more decrepit than at the Samuel. The clanking of walkers echoes in the hallways.

My presence puts delighted smiles on all the old ladies' faces. Some even take the liberty of shaking my hand.

"You're a very handsome young man, sir."

At the Manoir Saint-Sacrement, I am a supermodel. I am Jude Law, Aladdin, Leonardo DiCaprio. I am Yann Moreau.

Matante Pauline struts about on my arm through the common areas. I feel like she wants to show me off to her neighbours. I stand out here for the sole fact that I'm under seventy years old. A bit of my popularity reflects on Pauline.

"You have a very handsome great-nephew, madame."

I'm a celebrity.

::

In her apartment with a view of the Laurentians, Matante Pauline pours me a glass of pear juice. Leave it to her to go with that beverage choice. It's totally tasteless.

She sinks into her pink armchair. She seems to be breathing more heavily than before. Sometimes, at the end of a sentence, she releases a long, wheezing sigh. Like at the Samuel Holland, all her walls are covered in paintings. But here, there are no boxes or plastic bags cluttering the furniture or the floor. My parents managed to get rid of her knick-knacks. On the other hand, in each corner of each room there's a small table topped with a little notebook and pen, and under each table, a small wastebasket. As if Matante Pauline, at any moment, might need to scribble a note and then throw it in the trash. I don't know if this is a new trend for old ladies. It's unclear to me.

"The people are kind to me: the nurses, the servers, the other residents . . . Almost no men, have you noticed? They're all dead. Women live longer than their husbands, it's natural. My neighbour on the floor, Mrs. Quirion, was married to a Béland from Neuville . . ."

With Matante Pauline, a story from the olden days is always close at hand. I don't mind. Comfortably, I settle into her words. I only have to smile and nod while the May sun moves across the linoleum floor of the living room.

"And you, my handsome Colin?"

And me?

"You're graduating soon. You always got good grades, always worked hard. Your parents are proud of you. We're all proud of you."

She looks at me tenderly; I don't know what to do with myself. I smile shyly and take a sip of juice.

: :

At the door of the residence, Matante Pauline gives me a kiss.

"It really made me happy, seeing you today. Come back whenever you like. Not much happens here, as you can see—everyone is deaf. Say hi to your family for me."

I nod and start to turn away, but she grabs my arm. "And Colin . . . do whatever you want to do."

I look up at her.

"Become whatever you want to be. Make a fine life for yourself. It goes so quickly."

Touched, I can't find the words to answer her. So I go on my way.

61

NEVER GET OFF

THE GOOD THING ABOUT THE FERRY between Quebec City and Lévis is that you can board it with a bus pass and stay on it all day. No one is watching; you can sit down in a corner and cross the river as many times as you want. You just don't get off.

It's June 6, and it's hot out. Yann Moreau and I are commandeering a bench on the boat's upper deck. My eyes move constantly from Cap Diamant to the Château Frontenac to the Séminaire de Québec to the tip of Île d'Orléans. I seldom look toward Lévis, where there isn't much to see aside from churches and small houses.

From time to time, my fingers slide between those of my boyfriend. If someone approaches, I remove my hand.

"Where will you live?"

Yann has been accepted into the film program. He's moving to Montreal at the end of August.

"At the university, in the dorms. At least for the first year. After that, I'll find roommates to share an apartment."

This summer, he'll be working as a lifeguard at his neighbourhood pool. I'll go swimming there as often as possible. As for me, I'm still unemployed. I have to give out more CVs. My parents have stopped bringing it up; they were so stressed out by Matante Pauline's move that they decided to let it go. In the end, they've decided it's okay that their almost seventeen-year-old son isn't working. According to them, I'll have lots of time to earn money later. They want me to take advantage of my youth. Maybe they're not wrong.

"Maybe I'll come join you in Montreal. We could live together."

"After you're done college? Yeah, maybe . . ."

Two school years loom between us—it might as well be a galaxy. I think about going back to school without Yann, to college, rudderless, to an autumn without warmth; I imagine him falling in love with someone else, forgetting about me as soon as he arrives in Montreal, a city that attracts all the boys like him, like us.

"You know, Colin, you have to do whatever interests you," he says.

"What do you mean?"

Silence.

"What do you mean?" I repeat.

"Just that we all have to pursue our own interests. I know that I want to study film, so I have to move to Montreal. But if Quebec City is where you want to be . . . You can't force yourself to join me."

What does this lack of enthusiasm mean? Doesn't he want me to move to Montreal? Tears well up in my eyes. He's breaking up with me. Is he breaking up with me? He's definitely breaking up with me. This is the beginning of the end. My voice quivering, I start to beg pathetically.

"Look, I know I'm not the most interesting guy in town. I know you could meet someone else tomorrow morning. I know I'm lucky to have you, I know . . . But I love you more than anything, and I don't want us to break up. I don't want us to think about that."

His arms encircle me. "That's not true, any of that. You *are* the most interesting guy in town. You're funny, sweet, brilliant, handsome . . . I love you, too. Forget it. There's no point thinking about what's to come. We'll find out as we go, we'll see."

What a coward! I need certainty. "No, we have to promise to call each other often, to write all the time. We have to promise to stay together!"

He sighs. "It's impossible to promise that, handsome. We won't be in the same city anymore. We just have to take things as they come. But I promise that I love you. Colin, I love you! Right here and now. Today, on the ferry, we love each other!"

I explode. "I know, but we're going to get off eventually!"

My god, I'm bawling like Rose on the Titanic when she jumps out of her lifeboat, determined to drown with Jack. I have never been in so much pain, but I've never felt so alive. Something is vibrating inside me; something is humming with excitement.

Overcome with passion, we kiss, with no regard for the other passengers. When we finally get off the ferry, we walk to the Upper Town in silence. At Place D'Youville, he climbs aboard the 25, and I take the 7.

On the bus, I cling to my Discman. "Pour que tu m'aimes encore" plays on a loop, the soundtrack to my inner turmoil, all the way to Sainte-Foy. Eyes closed, I doze off to images from the video: Céline, barefoot in her little white dress, doing a tarot reading, casting a spell on a marionette and setting fire to her witch's hut. To hold onto their lovers, superstars like her have access to the best magic spells of the most powerful witch doctors in Africa.

I am depleted. Love is a cinematic production.

62

DON'T EVER CHANGE

SINCE THE AFTERNOON ON THE FERRY, nothing matters to me anymore. I've decided to stop feeling. Yann Moreau loves me and I love him, but he'll be leaving soon. How can I fully embrace this pain, other than alone or with Eugénie? I know I'll be existing for a sign, a message, a phone call or a visit from Yann. The summer will be short and depressing. Between now and September, my sky can only narrow. I would rather go through this period detached.

So when Clément said to me this morning, "It's your prom tonight, Col! And tomorrow is your birthday! Are you excited? You're almost a man!" I didn't even look at him. I feel like I'll never quite be a man.

The day went by quickly. In the afternoon, assisted by my father, I put on my suit, knotted my tie, combed my hair in a slightly different way. In front of the bathroom mirror, I said, "So this is what I'll look like at my prom."

Like a teenager who works in a bank.

: :

Marie-Louise, Daniel and I go over to Eugénie's for a photo session in the garden. It's cloudy but warm.

As usual, Liette is laughing when she opens the door. "Sorry, Michel was just telling me a joke! Come in, come in! Hi!"

To fit in with the Bujold family mood, my parents make a few funny comments to prolong the fun. Then, from the living room, Eugénie appears.

Majestic in her red floozie dress. A cascade of curls on top of her head. And around her neck, the Heart of the Ocean!

I am speechless. Proud of her surprise, she raises the blue heart from her chest.

"Look! My father went to get it at the knick-knack shop in Lévis. The saleswoman couldn't believe someone was buying it. I thought the blue would be pretty with my red dress."

She really looks like Kate Winslet descending the grand first-class staircase in *Titanic*. I am amazed.

"It's beautiful! It's incredibly beautiful!"

Behind me, my parents are smiling widely. Adults always find it cute when young people get all dressed up.

In the backyard, we stand near a bank of peonies in bloom. We put our arms around each other's waists, smile. Click, click. All combinations are captured: with the parents, without the parents, as a family, as a couple . . . My mother strokes my back frequently, a faraway look in her eyes.

Then Eugénie and I get into my father's car.

::

Some students have rented limousines; others are driven in Mercedes by their parents. In a parallel world, a better world, Yann Moreau would have escorted me to prom, and we would have arrived in his mother's BMW. But instead, my date and I are dropped off at the front door of a hotel in Old Quebec by my father's Toyota.

I don't know which way to turn in this rainbow procession of dresses. All the girls are stunning. Next to them, the guys look dull and square in their bankers' uniforms. Without the girls, prom would seem like a convention of young psychopaths.

Eugénie takes my arm. We enter the ballroom. Heads turn; everyone is looking at my friend. She is radiant.

At the dinner, between two mouthfuls of chicken in sauce, I am surprised to find myself having a good time. Catherine Crosnier and Guillaume Brassard, seated near us, are talking to me. Everyone is in a good mood. It's like the cliques no longer exist. After dessert, Catherine Wagner hosts a sort of comedy-laced ceremony during which the popular students give each other awards while cracking inside jokes into the microphone.

At one point, Guillaume Hervé drags his chair over to our table and starts chatting with Eugénie, laughing very loudly. He even touches her dress. I don't understand his behaviour at all.

"I kissed him at Guillaume Arteau's party. After you left," my friend finally whispers in my ear.

My jaw drops. "And you've been hiding this from me for two months?"

"Relax, Colin, you're not the only one with secrets. We just kissed. But I have to admit, he looks really fucking hot tonight."

Guillaume Hervé is wearing a suit similar to mine, but he's removed his jacket to reveal black suspenders over his white shirt. He does look hot.

My gosh! Michel and Liette were right: their daughter might end up sleeping with a guy in her Laura Petites red dress. Good for her. My best friend deserves to have great sex with the person of her choice.

::

Against all expectations, prom pulls me out of my funk. I've stopped thinking about Yann's departure and our shaky future. On the dance floor, I jump all over the place, holding Eugénie by the shoulders. We laugh like mad. I forget about everything.

At the end of the evening, the yearbooks are passed around. Friendships and resentments no longer exist; we sign the books blindly, in an attempt to leave a trace of ourselves in the memories of the others, all the others.

I notice the same type of message coming up over and over:

Don't ever change! Stay exactly the way you are!
You're amazing!

It astounds me that Guillaume Dionne, Guillaume Langlois, Catherine Pronovost and Catherine Laramée all tell me to never change, when they don't have the slightest idea who I am. But my astonishment doesn't prevent me from joining in; lacking inspiration, I accompany my signature with the same kind of empty advice.

I'd prefer if they wrote:

Please change! Don't stay like this!
You have problems!

That would also be my advice to the others. Frankly, that's what I wish for us all. If none of these teenagers ever change as adults, there is little hope for society.

When I confide my reservations to Eugénie, she looks at me, wide-eyed. "You're so negative!"

I go from one surprise to the next; Guillaume Piché walks over to me and strikes up a conversation as naturally as anything, like we were the same, like high school was only a timid prelude to a healthy friendship.

It's only the imminent dissolution of our grade that's fostering this friendly atmosphere. I have nothing against it, but I can't participate in it. Are these moments of togetherness supposed to erase from my memory five years of listening to these guys snicker and call each other gay?

At the hotel exit, I run into Catherine Julien, elegant in a Japanese-inspired purple dress. I smile and wave at her. She looks away. She's right. My small, friendly gestures could never make up for the brutality of her high school years.

::

I'm not going to the after-party. I signed up for it, but I've changed my mind. I'm worried I'd feel the way I did at Guillaume Arteau's party. I don't belong there.

Before leaving Eugénie, I hug her tightly. "I love you."

She takes off the Heart of the Ocean and places it around my neck.

"I'm afraid I'll lose it at the after-party."

Bursting with joy, she goes off to join Guillaume Hervé. I touch the huge imitation sapphire hanging outside my shirt. Even fake, it's a hefty piece of jewellery.

On the sidewalk, I head in the direction of Place D'Youville.

63

IT'S ALL COMING BACK TO ME NOW

IT'S AFTER ELEVEN O'CLOCK. On rue Saint-Jean, groups of Saturday night partygoers pass me, laughing. The air is mild; the night smells like summer. In one hour, I'll be seventeen years old.

I got through it. I escaped it. Childhood, adolescence. High school. Starting tomorrow, my time is my own. I am entering the adult world. The real world.

At rue Sainte-Angèle I come across a gang of drunk guys. They're making a spectacle of themselves, shouting nonsense. I give them a wide berth. But two of them decide that I am part of the act. They block my way, lean into my face. "Yeah, definitely a fag, guys!" they cry.

And they move off. Just like that, untroubled, without remorse. The world is their oyster. They travel through it, leaving traces of their passage here and there. They'll never think about me again. They've already forgotten me.

I am trembling. I dig deep for a lesson I can draw from their attack, a mistake I can correct.

It's the Heart of the Ocean that triggered them, of course. I should have hidden it under my shirt. It was my appearance that attracted their attention. But also probably the way I walked, looked and breathed that set them off. In any case, once again I let down my guard. Tears well up in my eyes. I keep on moving, hoping no one else notices me.

At the Saint-Jean Gate, a telephone booth illuminates a piece of the sidewalk. I need to talk to my parents. To hear their voices, to hear love and security, to hear "Stay where you are, we're coming to get you." I rummage in my pockets for a coin; nothing. I think about robbing the homeless guy sleeping nearby, against the fortifications.

On the ramparts, I find a quiet spot to sit down and burst into tears.

: :

My trembling has quieted down. One hand on the jewel hanging from my neck, I take deep breaths. At my feet, Quebec City extends to the west. Tonight, it appears to me exactly as it revealed itself, as it welcomed me: full of raging tigers. I haven't seen anything yet.

Behind me, a car slowly climbs rue D'Auteuil. Its windows are lowered. I can clearly hear the song that's playing:

If you forgive me all this
If I forgive you all that
We forgive and forget
And it's all coming back to me
When you see me like this
And when I see you like that
We see just what we want to see
All coming back to me
The flesh and the fantasies
All coming back to me
I can barely recall
But it's all coming back to me now

For a few moments, miraculously, Céline Dion's invincible voice buries the broken soundtrack of the year I was sixteen. In five minutes, I'll be seventeen.

To give myself a shot of courage, I think about Yann and Eugénie. With them, I'm not entirely alone, even though I'm often angry and afraid; even though it's all—the joy and the sorrow, the pride and the shame—coming back to me now.

I walk back down the hill to face the city.

QC FICTION

NOTABLE TITLES FROM QC FICTION

MOREL, A NOVEL
by Maxime Raymond Bock
translated by Mélissa Bull
Finalist, 2024 Governor General's Literary Award for Translation

IT'S ALL COMING BACK TO ME NOW
by Jean-Michel Fortier
translated by Jonathan Kaplansky

SONGS FOR THE COLD OF HEART
by Eric Dupont
translated by Peter McCambridge
Finalist, 2018 Giller Prize
Finalist, 2018 Governor General's Literary Award for Translation

ROSA'S VERY OWN PERSONAL REVOLUTION
by Eric Dupont
translated by Peter McCambridge
Winner, 2023 Governor General's Literary Award for Translation

TATOUINE
by Jean-Christophe Réhel
translated by Katherine Hastings & Peter McCambridge

ALL KIDDING ASIDE
by Jean-Christophe Réhel
translated by Neil Smith
Finalist for 2025 Foreword Indies Award

Baraka Books

NOTABLE TITLES FROM BARAKA BOOKS

MY THIEVERY OF THE PEOPLE
Stories by Leila Marshy
Winner of the 2025 Danuta Gleed Award for Short Fiction

EYES HAVE SEEN, FROM MISSISSIPPI TO MONTREAL
A Memoir by Fred Anderson
Finalist, 2025 Concordia First Book Award
Silver Winner, 2025 Foreword Indies Award

NORTHERN GIRLS
by Michelle Willms

THE GUILT TRIPPERS
by Philippe Mineau

MIX
Paper
FSC® C100212

Printed by Imprimerie Gauvin
Gatineau, Québec